HARPERCOLLINS CHILDREN'S

Stories
for

Year Olds

HARPERCOLLINS CHILDREN'S

Stories
for

Year Olds

Compiled by Julia Eccleshare

HarperCollins *Children's Books*

First published in the United Kingdom by HarperCollins, Young Lions, in 1991 as
Tobie and the Face Merchant and Other Stories for Six-Year-Olds
Published in this revised edition by HarperCollins *Children's Books* in 2022
HarperCollins *Children's Books* is a division of HarperCollins*Publishers* Ltd
1 London Bridge Street
London SE1 9GF

www.harpercollins.co.uk

HarperCollins*Publishers*
Macken House, 39/40 Mayor Street Upper
Dublin 1, D01 C9W8, Ireland

2

ISBN 978–0–00–852470–8

A CIP catalogue record for this title is available from the British Library.

Typeset in 13/24pt ITC Century Std by
Palimpsest Book Production Ltd, Falkirk, Stirlingshire

Printed and bound in the UK using 100% renewable electricity
at CPI Group (UK) Ltd

MIX
Paper | Supporting
responsible forestry
FSC
www.fsc.org
FSC™ C007454

This book is produced from independently certified FSC™ paper
to ensure responsible forest management.

Find out more about HarperCollins and the environment at
www.harpercollins.co.uk/green

Contents

It's a Dog's Life

Michael Morpurgo
Illustrated by Penny Bell

Open one eye.
Same old basket, same old kitchen.
Another day.

Ear's itching.
Have a good scratch.
Lovely.

Have a good stretch.

Here comes Lula.

'Morning, Russ,' she says.

'Do you know what day it is today?'

Silly question! Course I do!

It's the day after yesterday

and the day before tomorrow.

Out I go. Smarty's barking his 'good morning' at

me from across the valley.

Good old Smarty. Best friend I've got, except

Lula of course.

I bark mine back.

I can't hang about. Got to get the cows in.

There they are.

Lula's dad likes me to

have them ready for milking

by the time he gets there.

Better watch that one with the new calf.

She's a bit skippy.

Lie down, nose in the grass.

Give her the hard eye.

There she goes, in amongst the rest.

And here comes Lula's dad singing his way

down to the dairy.

'Good dog,' he says.

I wag my tail. He likes that.

He gives me another 'good dog'.

I get my milk. Lovely.

Off back up to the house.

Well, I don't want to miss my breakfast, do I?

Lula's already scoffing her bacon and eggs.

I sit down next to her

and give her my

very best begging look.

It always works.

Two bacon rinds in secret under the table,

and all her toast crusts too. Lovely.

There's good pickings

under the baby's chair this morning.

I hoover it all up. Lovely.

Lula always likes me to go with her

to the end of the lane.

She loves a bit of a cuddle, and
a lick or two before the school bus comes.

'Oh, Russ,' she whispers. 'A horse.
It's all I want for my birthday.'
And I'm thinking, *'Scuse me, what's so great
about a horse?*
Isn't a dog good enough?

Then along comes the bus and on she gets.
'See you,' she says.

Lula's dad is whistling for me.
'Where are you, you old rascal you?'

I'm coming.
I'm coming.

Back up the lane,

through the hedge,

over the gate.

'Don't just sit there, Russ.

I want those sheep in for shearing.'

And all the while he keeps on

with his whistling and whooping.

I mean, does he think

I haven't done this before?

Doesn't he know

this is what I'm made for?

Hare down the hill.

Leap the stream.

Get right around behind them.

Keep low. Don't rush them. That's good.

They're all going now. The whole flock of them
are trotting along nicely.
And I'm slinking along behind, my eye on every
one of them,
my bark and my bite deep inside their heads.

'Good dog,' I get. Third one today. Not bad.

I watch the shearing
from the top of the haybarn.
Good place to sleep, this.

Tigger's somewhere here.
I can smell her.

There she is, up on the rafter,

waving her tail at me.

She's teasing me. I'll show her.

Later, I'll do it later.

Sleep now. Lovely.

'Russ! Where are you, Russ?

I want these sheep out.

Now! Move yourself.'

All right, all right.

Down I go, and out they go,

all in a great muddle

bleating at each other,

bopping one another.

They don't recognise each other without their

clothes on.

Not very bright, that's the trouble with sheep.

Will you look at that!

There's hundreds of crows out in my corn field.

Well, I'm not having that, am I?

After them! Show them who's boss!

Thirsty work, this.

What's this? Fox!

I can smell him.

I follow him down

through the bluebell wood to his den.

He's down there, deep down.

Can't get at him. Pity.

Need a drink.

Shake myself dry in the sun.

Time for another sleep.

Lovely.

Smarty wakes me.

I know what he's thinking.

How about

a Tigger hunt?

We find her soon enough.

We're after her.

We're catching her up.

Closer. Closer.

Right on her tail.

That's not fair.

She's found a tree.

Up she goes.

We can't climb trees, so we bark our heads off.

Ah well, you can't win them all.

'Russ, where were you, Russ?'

Lula's dad. Shouting for me again.

'Get those calves out in the field.

What's the point in keeping a dog

and barking myself?'

Nothing worse than trying to move young calves.

They're all tippy-toed and skippy.

Pretty things.

Pity they get so big and lumpy when they get

older.

There, done it. Well done, me!

Back to the end of the lane to meet Lula.
I'm a bit late. She's there already,
swinging her bag and singing.

'Happy birthday to me,
happy birthday to me.
Happy birthday, dear Lula,
happy birthday to me!'

For tea there's a big cake with candles on it,
and they're singing that song again.
Will you look at them
tucking into that cake!
And never a thought for me.

Lula's so busy unwrapping her presents

that she doesn't even notice I'm there,

not even when I put my head on her knee.

Car! Car coming up my lane, and not one I know.

I'm out of the house in a flash.

I'm not just a farm dog, you know, I'm a guard

dog too.

'Russ! Stop that barking, will you?'

That's all the thanks I get.

I'm telling you, it's a dog's life.

Looks like a horse to me.

Give him a sniff.

Yes, definitely a horse.

Lula goes mad.

She's hugging the horse

just like she hugs me, only for longer.

A lot longer.

'He's beautiful,' she's saying.

'Just what I wanted.'

Well, I'm not staying where I'm not wanted.

I haven't had any of that cake,

and they're not watching.

Nip back inside. Jump on a chair.

I'm a champion chomper.

Ooops.

The plate's fallen off the table.

I'm in trouble now.

They all come running in.

I look dead innocent.

Doesn't fool them, though.

'You rascal, you. Out you go!'

I don't care. It was worth it.

I go and sit at the top of the hill

and tell Smarty all about it.

He barks back, 'Good on you!

Who wants to be a good dog, anyway?'

Then Lula's sitting down beside me.

'I really love my horse,' she says,

'but I love you more, Russ. Promise.'

Give her a good lick. Make her giggle.

I like it when she giggles.

Lick her again.

Lovely.

The High Hills

Jill Barklem

For many generations, families of mice have made their homes in the roots and trunks of the trees of Brambly Hedge, a dense and tangled hedgerow that borders the field on the other side of the stream.

The Brambly Hedge mice lead busy lives.

During the fine weather, they collect flowers, fruits, berries and nuts from the Hedge and surrounding fields, and prepare delicious jams, pickles and preserves that are kept safely in the Store Stump for the winter months ahead.

Although the mice work hard, they make time for fun too. All through the year, they mark the seasons with feasts and festivities and, whether it be a little mouse's birthday, an eagerly awaited wedding or the first day of spring, the mice welcome the opportunity to meet and celebrate.

It was the very end of autumn. The weather was damp and chilly and Wilfred was spending the day inside with the weavers. *Clickety, clack* went the loom, *whirr, whirr* went the spinning wheel. Lily and Flax were in a hurry.

'We must finish in time,' said Flax. 'We promised Mr Apple.'

'What are you making?' asked Wilfred.

'Blankets,' replied Lily.

'Who are they for?' said Wilfred.

'They are for the voles in the High Hills,' replied Flax. 'They have just discovered that the moths have eaten all their quilts and they've no time to make new ones before the cold weather comes. They're too busy gathering stores for winter. We're helping out.'

'Can I help too?' asked Wilfred.

'That's kind of you, Wilfred, but not just now,' said Lily. 'Why don't you find yourself a book to read while I finish spinning this wool?'

Wilfred went over to the bookcase. On a shelf, tucked between volumes on dyestuffs and

27

weaves, he found a thick book called *Daring Explorers of Old Hedge Days*. He settled himself comfortably and began to turn the pages.

'Sir Hogweed Horehound,' he read, 'determined to conquer the highest peak of the High Hills, for there, he knew, he would discover gold. Alone he set forth, taking in his trusty pack all he needed to survive the rigorous journey . . .'

Wilfred sat entranced. The whirr of the spinning wheel became the swish of eagles' wings, the clatter of the loom, the sound of falling rock, and the drops of rain on the window, jewels from the depths of some forgotten cave. Was there really gold in the hills beyond Brambly Hedge, he wondered.

Suddenly a door slammed. It was his mother come to fetch him home for tea.

'I hope he hasn't been too much trouble,' said Mrs Toadflax.

'He has been so quiet, we'd almost forgotten he was here,' said Lily. 'You can send him down again tomorrow if you like.'

Lily and Flax were already hard at work when Wilfred arrived the next morning. He settled down by the window again to read about Sir Hogweed Horehound and his intrepid search for gold.

The morning flew past and by the time Mr Apple arrived to collect Wilfred, Flax and Lily had almost finished the cloth.

'I'm sorry we couldn't match the yellow,' said Flax. 'We've used the last of Grandpa Blackthorn's lichen and no other dye will do.'

'Never mind,' said Mr Apple. 'It's the

blankets they need. We'll take them up to the hills tomorrow.'

'The hills,' repeated Wilfred. 'Are you really going up to the High Hills?'

'Yes,' replied Mr Apple. 'Why?'

'Can I come?' Wilfred asked desperately. 'Please say I can.'

'Oh, I don't think so,' said Mr Apple. 'It's too far. We shall have to stay overnight.'

'I'll be very good,' urged Wilfred.

Mr Apple relented. 'We'll see if your mother agrees,' he said. 'Come on, young mouse. It's time to go home.

To Wilfred's surprise, his mother did agree.

'It will do him good to be in the open air,' she said. Wilfred rushed upstairs to pack. He knew just what he would need. Sir Hogweed

Horehound had listed all the essential gear in his book: rope, a whistle, food, firesticks, cooking pots, a groundsheet and blankets, a spoon, a water bottle and a first-aid kit.

'And I had better have a special bag for the gold,' said Wilfred to himself as he gathered everything together.

He went to bed straight after supper. It was a long way to the High Hills and to get to the Voles' Hole by dusk, they would have to make an early start.

Next morning, soon after dawn, Flax, Lily and Mr Apple called for Wilfred. They were carrying packs on their backs, full of cloth and blankets, and there was honey and cheese and a pudding for the voles from Mrs Apple. Wilfred hurried down the stairs.

'Whatever have you got there?' asked Flax.

'It's my essential gear,' explained Wilfred.

'You won't be needing a cooking pot. I've got some sandwiches,' said Mr Apple.

'But I must take everything,' said Wilfred. His lip began to quiver. 'How can I find gold without my equipment?'

'You'll have to carry it then,' said Mr Apple. 'We can't manage any more.'

The first part of the journey was easy. The four mice went up the hedge, past Crabapple Cottage, the Store Stump and Old Oak Palace. Then they rounded the weavers' cottages and arrived at the bank of the stream. Carefully they picked their way over the stepping stones and clambered up into the buttercup meadow.

Wilfred strode through the grass, occasionally lifting his paw to gaze at the distant peaks. Beyond the bluebell woods he could see the path begin to climb.

Mr Apple looked back. 'How's my young explorer?' he said. 'Ready for lunch?'

'Oh, please,' said Wilfred, easing off his pack with relief.

The mice ate their picnic and enjoyed the late autumn sunshine but soon it was time to go on. All through the afternoon they walked. The path became steeper and steeper, and when they looked behind them, they could see the fields and woods and hedges spread out far below.

By tea time, it was getting dark and cold, and the hills around were shrouded in mist. At last they saw a tiny light shining from a rock beneath an old hawthorn tree.

'Here we are,' said Mr Apple. 'Knock on the door, Wilfred, will you?'

An elderly vole opened it a crack. When she saw Mr Apple, she cried, 'Pip! Fancy you climbing all this way, and with your bad leg too.'

'We couldn't leave you without blankets, now could we,' said Mr Apple.

The mice crowded into the cottage and were soon sitting round the fire, drinking hot bilberry soup and resting their weary paws.

For Wilfred, the conversation came and went in drifts and soon he was fast asleep. Someone lifted him gently on to a little bracken bed in the corner and the next thing he knew was the delicious smell of breakfast, sizzling on the range.

Wilfred ate heartily, oatcakes with rowanberry jelly, and listened to the voles describing their hard life in the hills. He was disappointed when Mr Apple announced that it was time to leave.

'Can't we explore a bit first?' he begged.

'Flax and I have to get back to work,' said Lily, 'but why don't you two follow on later?'

'Well,' relented Mr Apple, 'there are some fine junipers beyond the crag . . .'

'And Mrs Apple *loves* junipers,' said Wilfred quickly, 'let's get her some.'

So the mice said goodbye to the voles and Mr Apple and Wilfred set off up the path.

Wilfred ran on ahead and was soon round the crag. When Mr Apple caught up with him, Wilfred was half way up a steep face of rock.

'Wilfred!' cried Mr Apple. 'Come down.'

'Just a minute,' shouted Wilfred. 'I've found something.'

Mr Apple watched as Wilfred pulled himself

up on to the narrow ledge and started scraping at the rock and stuffing something in his pocket.

'Look!' cried Wilfred. 'Gold!'

'Don't be silly, Wilfred,' shouted Mr Apple. 'That's not gold. Come down at once.'

Wilfred looked over the side. His voice faltered. 'I can't,' he said. 'I'm scared.'

Mr Apple was exasperated. 'Wait there,' he shouted. Slowly he climbed the steep rocks, carefully placing his paws in the clefts of the stones. The ledge was very narrow. 'We'll edge along this way. Perhaps the two paths will meet,' he said. 'We certainly can't go down the way we came up.'

As they walked cautiously along the ledge, an ominous mist began to rise from the valley.

'If only we had some rope,' said Mr Apple. 'We ought to rope ourselves together.'

Wilfred put his paw in his pack and produced the rope! Mr Apple tied it carefully round Wilfred's middle and then round his own. And it was just as well for a few minutes later they were engulfed in a thick white fog.

'Turn to the rock face, Wilfred, we'll ease our way along, one step at a time.'

They went on for a long time, then they took a rest. As they sat on the wet rock, the mist parted for a few seconds, just long enough to show a deep strange valley below.

Mr Apple was worried. He had no idea where they were. It looked as though they would have to spend the night on the mountain. It would be very cold and dark, and all he had in his pocket were two sandwiches the voles had given him for the journey down. His leg was feeling stiff and sore too. What was to be done? He explained the situation to Wilfred.

'It's all my fault,' said Wilfred, 'I didn't mean us to get lost. I just wanted to find gold like Sir Hogweed.'

'Never mind,' said Mr Apple. 'We must look for somewhere to spend the night.'

A short way along the path, the ledge became a little wider. Under an overhang of rock a small cave ran back into the mountainside.

'Look,' cried Wilfred, slinging his pack inside. 'Base camp!'

Mr Apple sat gingerly on the damp moss at the mouth of the cave. Everything felt damp, his clothes, his whiskers, his handkerchief.

'I wish I'd brought my pipe, we could have

made a fire,' he sighed. 'Never mind, we'll huddle close and try to keep warm.'

But Wilfred was busily searching in his pack again. Out came the firesticks and the tinderbox. 'I'll see if there's some dry wood at the back of the cave,' he said enthusiastically.

'Wilfred,' cried Mr Apple in admiration, 'you're a real explorer.'

Soon they had a cheerful blaze on the ledge outside the cave. Wilfred produced two blankets and the mice wrapped themselves up snugly while their clothes dried in front of the fire. The little kettle was filled from the water bottle and proudly Wilfred set out a feast of bread and cheese and honeycakes.

'You know,' said Mr Apple, as he settled back against the rock, 'I haven't enjoyed a meal so much for years.'

To while away the time, Mr Apple began to tell Wilfred stories of his adventurous youth, and as they talked, the mists gradually cleared and a starry sky spread out above them. All was quiet but for the murmur of a stream which ran through the valley below like a silver ribbon in the moonlight. Warmed by the fire, they became drowsy and soon fell asleep.

The next morning they were woken by the sun shining into the cave.

'It's a beautiful day,' called Wilfred, peering over the ledge, 'and I can see a path down the mountain.'

Mr Apple sat up and stretched his leg. It still hurt. 'We'll have to go down slowly, I'm afraid,' he said.

'Is it your leg?' said Wilfred. 'I can help,' and he brought out a jar of comfrey ointment from his first-aid kit.

They packed up and set off down the path. Mr Apple did the best he could but his leg was very painful. He managed to get as far as the stream but then he stopped and sat on a boulder with a sigh. 'I can't go any further,' he said. 'What are we to do?'

The two mice sat in silence and watched the water swirl past the bank.

'Don't worry,' said Wilfred, trying to be cheerful. 'We'll think of something.'

Suddenly he jumped up. 'I've got it,' he cried excitedly. 'We'll *sail* down the stream!' He ran to the bank and with his ice axe, he hooked out some large sticks that had caught behind a rock in the water. Using his rope to lash them together, he made a raft. 'Come on,' said Wilfred, 'we'll shoot the rapids!'

'Are you sure this is a good idea?' said Mr Apple. 'Wherever will we end up?'

'Don't worry,' said Wilfred. 'It's all going to be all right.'

Carefully they climbed on to the raft, Mr Apple let go of the bank and they were off!

They were swept to the middle of the stream as it raced down the mountainside, twisting and turning, sweeping and splashing, careering over rocks and cutting through deep banks.

'My hat,' shouted Wilfred. 'I've lost my hat.'

'Never mind that,' cried Mr Apple, 'just hold on tight. There's a boulder ahead.'

Wilfred gripped the sides of the raft, and somehow they managed to keep the raft, and themselves, afloat.

Down by the stream, Dusty was ferrying a search party of mice over to the buttercup meadows when he suddenly caught sight of a small red hat floating along on the current.

'Look there,' he shouted. All the mice peered over the side of the boat.

'It's Wilfred's hat,' cried out Mrs Toadflax. 'Whatever can have happened to him?'

'Can he swim?' asked Mrs Apple anxiously.

Meanwhile, Wilfred and Mr Apple were beginning to enjoy their trip on the river. The ground had levelled out and the pace of the stream had become gentler. They looked about them with interest.

'Wilfred,' called Mr Apple, 'can you see

what I can see? I'm sure that's our willow ahead.'

Wilfred stared at the bank. 'It is!' he yelled.

'And there's the Old Oak Palace and the hornbeam. This is *our* stream!'

As they rounded the bend, they saw the Brambly Hedge mice climbing out of Dusty's boat. At the very same moment, Mrs Apple looked up and cried, 'Look! Look! There they are!'

The mice turned in amazement; the raft was almost abreast of them.

'Quick,' shouted Dusty, 'catch hold of this rope and I'll haul you to shore.'

As the two mice clambered out of the raft and up on to the bank, they all hugged each other.

'Wilfred, you're safe,' cried Mrs Toadflax.

'My dear, what has happened to your leg?' said Mrs Apple.

Lord Woodmouse took charge. 'Come on, everybody,' he said. 'Let's get these travellers home and dry, and then we can hear the full story.'

The mice made their way along the hedgerow to the hornbeam tree. Soon everybody was sitting round the fire, eating cake and drinking acorn coffee. 'Now tell us exactly what happened,' urged Flax.

'Well, it was my fault,' explained Wilfred again. 'I was looking for gold and I got stuck. Mr Apple had to rescue me and then we got lost. And Mr Apple's leg hurt so much, we had to come back on the raft.'

'Did you find any gold?' interrupted Primrose.

'No, only this silly old dust,' said Wilfred,

pulling the bag out of his pocket. Flax and Lily gasped.

'Wilfred! That's not dust. That's Grandpa Blackthorn's lichen. It's very rare. You *are* clever! Wherever did you find it?'

Primrose ran to fetch some paper and Wilfred proudly drew a map so that they could find the place again.

'And when we go, you shall come with us, Wilfred,' promised Lily.

Mr Apple was tired and soon he and Mrs Apple went home to Crabapple Cottage. One by one, the visitors drifted away. It was time for the explorer to go to bed.

Wilfred followed his mother up the stairs.

'What adventures!' she said, washing his face and paws and helping him take off his muddy dungarees.

Wilfred climbed into his bed. As his mother tucked him in, he thought of his night beneath the stars and snuggling down under his warm blankets, he was soon fast asleep.

Mary Poppins: East Wind

P. L. Travers
Illustrated by Mary Shephard

If you want to find Cherry Tree Lane all you have to do is ask the Policeman at the crossroads. He will push his helmet slightly to one side, scratch his head thoughtfully, and then he will point his huge white-gloved finger and say: 'First to your right, second to your left, sharp right again, and you're there. Good morning.'

And sure enough, if you follow his directions exactly, you *will* be there – right in the middle of Cherry Tree Lane, where the houses run down one side and the Park runs down the other and the cherry trees go dancing right down the middle.

If you are looking for Number Seventeen – and it is more than likely that you will be, for this book is all about that particular house – you will very soon find it. To begin with, it is the smallest house in the Lane. And, besides that, it is the only one that is rather dilapidated and needs a coat of paint. But Mr Banks, who owns it, said to Mrs Banks that she could have either a nice, clean, comfortable house or four children. But not both, for he couldn't afford it.

And after Mrs Banks had given the matter some consideration she came to the conclusion that she would rather have Jane, who was the eldest, and Michael, who came next, and John and Barbara, who were Twins and came last of all. So it was settled, and that was how the Banks family came to live at Number Seventeen, with Mrs Brill to cook for them, and Ellen to lay the tables, and Robertson Ay to cut the lawn and clean the knives and polish the shoes and, as Mr Banks always said, 'to waste his time and my money.'

And, of course, besides these there was Katie Nanna, who doesn't really deserve to come into the book at all because, at the time I am speaking of, she had just left Number Seventeen.

'Without a by your leave or a word of

warning. And what am I to do?' said Mrs Banks.

'Advertise, my dear,' said Mr Banks, putting on his shoes. 'And I wish Robertson Ay would go without a word of warning, for he has again polished one boot and left the other untouched. I shall look very lopsided.'

'That,' said Mrs Banks, 'is not of the least importance. You haven't told me what I'm to do about Katie Nanna.'

'I don't see how you can do anything about her since she has disappeared,' replied Mr Banks. 'But if it were me – I mean I – well, I should get somebody to put in the *Morning Paper* the news that Jane and Michael and John and Barbara Banks (to say nothing of their mother) require the best possible Nannie at the lowest possible wage and at once. Then

I should wait and watch for the Nannies to queue up outside the front gate, and I should get very cross with them for holding up the traffic and making it necessary for me to give the policeman a shilling for putting him to so much trouble. Now I must be off. Whew, it's as cold as the North Pole. Which way is the wind blowing?'

And, as he said that, Mr Banks popped his head out of the window and looked down the Lane to Admiral Boom's house at the corner. This was the grandest house in the Lane, and the Lane was very proud of it because it was built exactly like a ship. There was a flagstaff in the garden, and on the roof was a gilt weathercock shaped like a telescope.

'Ha!' said Mr Banks, drawing in his head very quickly. 'Admiral's telescope says East

Wind. I thought as much. There is frost in my bones. I shall wear two overcoats.' And he kissed his wife absentmindedly on one side of her nose and waved to the children and went away to the City.

Now, the City was a place where Mr Banks went every day – except Sundays, of course, and Bank Holidays – and while he was there he sat on a large chair in front of a large desk and made money. All day long he worked, cutting out pennies and shillings and half-crowns and threepenny-bits. And he brought them home with him in his little black bag. Sometimes he would give some to Jane and Michael for their money boxes, and when he couldn't spare any he would say, 'The Bank is broken,' and they would know he hadn't made much money that day.

Well, Mr Banks went off with his black bag, and Mrs Banks went into the drawing room and sat there all day long writing letters to the papers and begging them to send some Nannies to her at once as she was waiting; and upstairs in the Nursery, Jane and Michael watched at the window and wondered who would come. They were glad Katie Nanna had gone, for they had never liked her. She was old and fat and smelt of barley water. Anything, they thought, would be better than Katie Nanna – if not *much* better.

When the afternoon began to die away behind the Park, Mrs Brill and Ellen came to give them their supper and to bath the Twins. And after supper Jane and Michael sat at the window watching for Mr Banks to come home, and listening to the sound of the East Wind

blowing through the naked branches of the cherry trees in the Lane. The trees themselves, turning and bending in the half light, looked as though they had gone mad and were dancing their roots out of the ground.

'There he is!' said Michael, pointing suddenly to a shape that banged heavily against the gate. Jane peered through the gathering darkness.

'That's not Daddy,' she said. 'It's somebody else.'

Then the shape, tossed and bent under the wind, lifted the latch of the gate, and they could see that it belonged to a woman, who was holding her hat on with one hand and carrying a bag in the other. As they watched, Jane and Michael saw a curious thing happen. As soon as the shape was inside the gate the wind seemed to catch her up into the air and fling her at the house. It was as though it had flung her first at the gate, waited for her to open it, and then lifted and thrown her, bag and all, at the front door. The watching children heard a terrific bang, and as she landed the whole house shook.

'How funny! I've never seen that happen before,' said Michael.

'Let's go and see who it is!' said Jane, and taking Michael's arm she drew him away from the window, through the Nursery and out on to the landing. From there they always had a good view of anything that happened in the front hall.

Presently they saw their Mother coming out of the drawing room with a visitor following her. Jane and Michael could see that the newcomer had shiny black hair – 'Rather like a wooden Dutch doll,' whispered Jane. And that she was thin, with large feet and hands, and small, rather peering blue eyes.

'You'll find that they are very nice children,' Mrs Banks was saying.

Michael's elbow gave a sharp dig at Jane's ribs.

'And that they give no trouble at all,' continued Mrs Banks uncertainly, as if she herself didn't really believe what she was saying. They heard the visitor sniff as though *she* didn't either.

'Now, about references—' Mrs Banks went on.

'Oh, I make it a rule never to give references,' said the other firmly. Mrs Banks stared.

'But I thought it was usual,' she said. 'I mean – I understood people always did.'

'A very old-fashioned idea, to *my* mind,' Jane and Michael heard the stern voice say. '*Very* old-fashioned. *Quite* out of date, as you might say.'

Now, if there was one thing Mrs Banks did not like, it was to be thought old-fashioned. She just couldn't bear it. So she said quickly:

'Very well, then. We won't bother about them. I only asked, of course, in case *you* – er – required it. The nursery is upstairs—' And she led the way towards the staircase, talking all the time, without stopping once. And because she was doing that Mrs Banks did not notice what was happening behind her, but Jane and Michael, watching from the top landing, had an excellent view of the extraordinary thing the visitor now did.

Certainly she followed Mrs Banks upstairs, but not in the usual way. With her large bag in her hands she slid gracefully *up* the banisters, and arrived at the landing at the same time as Mrs Banks. Such a thing, Jane and Michael knew, had never been done before. Down, of course, for they had often done it themselves. But up – never! They gazed curiously at the strange new visitor.

'Well, that's all settled, then.' A sigh of relief came from the children's Mother.

'Quite. As long as *I'm* satisfied,' said the other, wiping her nose with a large red-and-white bandanna handkerchief.

'Why, children,' said Mrs Banks, noticing them suddenly, 'what are you doing there? This is your new nurse, Mary Poppins. Jane, Michael, say how do you do! And these' – she waved her hand at the babies in their cots – 'are the Twins.'

Mary Poppins regarded them steadily, looking from one to the other as though she were making up her mind whether she liked them or not.

'Will we do?' said Michael.

'Michael, don't be naughty,' said his Mother.

Mary Poppins continued to regard the four children searchingly. Then, with a long, loud sniff that seemed to indicate that she had made up her mind, she said:

'I'll take the position.'

'For all the world,' as Mrs Banks said to

her husband later, 'as though she were doing us a signal honour.'

'Perhaps she is,' said Mr Banks, putting his nose round the corner of the newspaper for a moment and then withdrawing it very quickly.

When their Mother had gone, Jane and Michael edged towards Mary Poppins, who stood, still as a post, with her hands folded in front of her.

'How did you come?' Jane asked. 'It looked just as if the wind blew you here.'

'It did,' said Mary Poppins briefly. And she proceeded to unwind her muffler from her neck and to take off her hat, which she hung on one of the bedposts.

As it did not seem as though Mary Poppins was going to say any more – though she sniffed a great deal – Jane, too, remained silent. But when she bent down to undo her bag, Michael could not restrain himself.

'What a funny bag!' he said, pinching it with his fingers.

'Carpet,' said Mary Poppins, putting her key in the lock.

'To carry carpets in, you mean?'

'No. Made of.'

'Oh,' said Michael. 'I see.' But he didn't – quite.

By this time the bag was open, and Jane and Michael were more than surprised to find it was completely empty.

'Why,' said Jane, 'there's nothing in it!'

'What do you mean – nothing?' demanded Mary Poppins, drawing herself up and looking as though she had been insulted. 'Nothing in it, did you say?'

And with that she took out from the empty bag a starched white apron and tied it round her waist. Next she unpacked a large cake of Sunlight Soap, a toothbrush, a packet of hairpins, a bottle of scent, a small folding armchair and a box of throat lozenges.

Jane and Michael stared.

'But I *saw*,' whispered Michael. 'I'm sure it was empty.'

'Hush!' said Jane, as Mary Poppins took out a large bottle labelled 'One Teaspoon to be Taken at Bedtime'.

A spoon was attached to the neck of the bottle, and into this Mary Poppins poured a dark crimson fluid.

'Is that your medicine?' enquired Michael, looking very interested.

'No, yours,' said Mary Poppins, holding out

the spoon to him. Michael stared. He wrinkled up his nose. He began to protest.

'I don't want it. I don't need it. I won't!'

But Mary Poppins's eyes were fixed upon him, and Michael suddenly discovered that you could not look at Mary Poppins and disobey her. There was something strange and extraordinary about her – something that was frightening and at the same time most exciting. The spoon came nearer. He held his breath, shut his eyes and gulped. A delicious taste ran round his mouth. He turned his tongue in it. He swallowed, and a happy smile ran round his face.

'Strawberry ice,' he said ecstatically. 'More, more, more!'

But Mary Poppins, her face as stern as before, was pouring out a dose for Jane. It ran into the spoon, silvery, greeny, yellowy. Jane tasted it.

'Lime-juice cordial,' she said, sliding her tongue deliciously over her lips. But when she saw Mary Poppins moving towards the Twins with the bottle Jane rushed at her.

'Oh, no – please. They're too young. It wouldn't be good for them. Please!'

Mary Poppins, however, took no notice, but, with a warning, terrible glance at Jane, tipped the spoon towards John's mouth. He lapped at it eagerly, and by the few drops that were spilt on his bib Jane and Michael could tell that the substance in the spoon this time was milk. Then Barbara had her share, and she gurgled and licked the spoon twice.

Mary Poppins then poured out another dose and solemnly took it herself.

'Rum punch,' she said, smacking her lips and corking the bottle.

Jane's eyes and Michael's popped with astonishment, but they were not given much time to wonder, for Mary Poppins, having put the miraculous bottle on the mantelpiece, turned to them.

'Now,' she said, 'spit-spot into bed.' And she began to undress them. They noticed that whereas buttons and hooks had needed all sorts of coaxing from Katie Nanna, for Mary Poppins they flew apart almost at a look. In less than a minute, they found themselves in bed and watching, by the dim light from the night light, the rest of Mary Poppins's unpacking being performed.

From the carpetbag she took out seven flannel nightgowns, four cotton ones, a pair of boots, a set of dominoes, two bathing caps and a postcard album. Last of all came a folding camp bedstead with blankets and eiderdown complete, and this she set down between John's cot and Barbara's.

Jane and Michael sat hugging themselves and watching. It was all so surprising that they could find nothing to say. But they knew, both of them, that something strange and wonderful had happened at Number Seventeen, Cherry Tree Lane.

Mary Poppins, slipping one of the flannel nightgowns over her head, began to undress underneath it as though it were a tent. Michael, charmed by this strange new arrival, unable to keep silent any longer, called to her.

'Mary Poppins,' he cried, 'you'll never leave us, will you?'

There was no reply from under the nightgown. Michael could not bear it.

'You won't leave us, will you?' he called anxiously.

Mary Poppins's head came out of the top of the nightgown. She looked very fierce.

'One word more from that direction,' she said threateningly, 'and I'll call the Policeman.'

'I was only saying,' began Michael, meekly, 'that we hoped you wouldn't be going away soon –' He stopped, feeling very red and confused.

Mary Poppins stared from him to Jane in silence. Then she sniffed.

'I'll stay till the wind changes,' she said shortly, and she blew out her candle and got into bed.

'That's all right,' said Michael, half to

himself and half to Jane. But Jane wasn't listening. She was thinking about all that had happened, and wondering . . .

And that is how Mary Poppins came to live at Number Seventeen, Cherry Tree Lane. And although they sometimes found themselves wishing for the quieter, more ordinary days when Katie Nanna ruled the household, everybody, on the whole, was glad of Mary Poppins's arrival. Mr Banks was glad because, as she arrived by herself and did not hold up the traffic, he had not had to tip the Policeman. Mrs Banks was glad because she was able to tell everybody that *her* children's nurse was so fashionable that she didn't believe in giving references. Mrs Brill and Ellen were glad because they could drink strong cups of tea all day in the kitchen and no longer needed to preside at nursery suppers. Robertson Ay was glad, too, because Mary Poppins had only one pair of shoes, and those she polished herself.

But nobody ever knew what Mary Poppins felt about it, for Mary Poppins never told anything . . .

Paddington's Good Turn

Michael Bond
Illustrated by R. W. Alley

Like most households up and down the country, number thirty-two Windsor Gardens had its own set routine.

In the case of the Brown family, Mr Brown usually went off to his office soon after breakfast, leaving Mrs Brown and Mrs Bird to go about their daily tasks. Most days, apart from the times when Jonathan and Judy were home for the school holidays, Paddington spent the morning visiting his friend Mr Gruber for cocoa and buns.

There were occasional upsets, of course, but on the whole the household was like an ocean liner. It steamed happily on its way, no matter what the weather.

So, when Mrs Bird returned home one day to what she fully expected to be an empty house and saw a strange face peering at her through the landing window, it took a moment or two to recover from the shock, and by then whoever it was had gone.

What made it far worse was the fact that she was halfway up the stairs to her bedroom at the time, which meant the face belonged to someone *outside* the house.

She hadn't seen any sign of a ladder on her way in; but all the same she rushed back downstairs again, grabbed the first weapon she could lay her hands on and dashed out into the garden.

Apart from a passing cat, which gave a loud shriek and scuttled off with its tail between its legs when it caught sight of her umbrella, everything appeared to be normal, so it was a mystery and no mistake.

When they heard the news later that day, Mr and Mrs Brown couldn't help wondering if Mrs Bird had been mistaken, but they didn't say so to her face in case she took umbrage.

'Perhaps it was a window cleaner gone to the wrong house,' suggested Mr Brown.

'In that case he made a very quick getaway,' said Mrs Bird. 'I wouldn't fancy having him do our windows.'

'I suppose it could have been a trick of the light,' said Mrs Brown.

Mrs Bird gave one of her snorts.

'I know what I saw,' she said darkly. 'And whatever it was, or *who*ever it was, they were up to no good.'

The Browns knew better than to argue, and Paddington, who had been given a detective outfit for his birthday, spent some time testing the windowsill for clues. Much to his disappointment, he couldn't find any marks on it other than his own. All the same, he took some measurements and carefully wrote the details down in his notebook.

In an effort to restore calm, Mr Brown rang

the police, but they were unable to be of much help either.

'It sounds to me like the work of 'Gentleman Dan, the Drainpipe Man',' said the officer who came to visit them. 'They do say he's usually in the Bahamas at this time of the year, but he could be back earlier than usual if the weather's bad.

'He didn't get his name for nothing. He bides his time until he sees what he thinks are some empty premises, and then he shins up the nearest drainpipe. He can be in and out of a house like a flash of lightning. Never leaves any trace of what we in the force call 'his dabs', on account of the fact that being a perfect gentleman he always wears gloves.'

The Browns felt they had done all they could to allay Mrs Bird's fears, but the officer left them with one final piece of advice.

'We shall be keeping a lookout in the area for the next few days,' he said, 'in case he strikes again. But if I were you, to be on the safe side, I'd invest in a can of Miracle non-dry, anti-burglar paint and give your downpipes a coat as soon as possible.

'It's available at all good do-it-yourself shops. Mark my words, you won't be troubled again, and if by any chance you are, the perpetrator will be so covered in black paint, he won't get very far before we pick him up.

'Not only that,' he said, addressing Mr Brown before driving off in his squad car, 'you may find you get a reduction on your insurance policy.'

'It sounds as though he's got shares in the company,' said Mr Brown sceptically, as he followed his wife back indoors. 'Either that or he has a spare-time job as one of their salesmen.'

'Henry!' exclaimed Mrs Brown.

In truth, the next day was a Friday, and after a busy week at the office Mr Brown had been looking forward to a quiet weekend. The thought of spending it up a ladder painting drainpipes was not high on his list of priorities.

In normal circumstances he might not have taken up Paddington's offer to help quite so readily.

'Are you sure it's wise?' asked Mrs Brown, when he told her. 'It's all very well Paddington saying bears are good at painting, but he says that about a lot of things. Remember what happened when he decorated the spare room.'

'That was years ago,' said Mr Brown. 'Anyway, the fact that he ended up wallpapering over the door and couldn't find his way out again had nothing to do with the actual painting. Besides, it's not as if it's something we shall be looking at all the time. Even Paddington can't do much harm painting a drainpipe.'

'I wouldn't be so sure,' warned Mrs Bird. 'Besides, it isn't just one drainpipe. There are at least half a dozen dotted round the house. And don't forget, it's non-dry paint. If that bear makes any mistakes, the marks will be there for ever more.'

'There must come a time when it dries off,' said Mr Brown optimistically.

'We could get Mr Briggs in,' suggested Mrs Brown, mentioning their local decorator. 'He's always ready to oblige.'

But Mr Brown's mind was made up, and when he arrived back from his office that evening he brought with him a large can of paint and an assortment of brushes.

Paddington was very excited when he saw them, and he couldn't wait to get started.

That night, he took the can of paint up to bed and read the small print on the side with the aid of a torch and the magnifying glass from his detective outfit.

According to the instructions, a lot of burglars climbed drainpipes in order to break into people's homes. In fact, the more he read, the more Paddington began to wonder why he had never seen one before; it sounded as though the streets must be full of them. There was even a picture of one on the back of the tin. He looked very pleased with himself as he slid down a pipe, a sack over his shoulder bulging with things he had taken. There was even a 'thinks balloon' attached to his head saying: 'Don't you wish you had done something about *your* pipes?'

Paddington opened his bedroom window and peered outside, but luckily there were no drainpipes anywhere near it, otherwise he might have tested the paint there and then, just to be on the safe side.

Before going to sleep he made out a list of all the other requirements ready for the morning. Something with which to open the tin; a wire brush for cleaning the pipes before starting work; a pair of folding steps – the instructions suggested it was only necessary to paint the bottom half of the pipe, there was no need to go all the way up to the top; and some white spirit to clean the brushes afterwards.

The following morning, as soon as breakfast was over, he waylaid Mrs Bird in the kitchen and persuaded her to let him have some plastic gloves and an old apron.

Knowing who would be landed with the task of getting any paint stains off his duffle coat if things went wrong, the Browns' housekeeper was only too willing to oblige.

'Mind you don't get any of that stuff on your whiskers,' she warned, as he disappeared out of the back door armed with his list. 'You don't want to spoil your elevenses.'

Paddington's suggestion that it might be a good idea to have them *before* he started work fell on deaf ears, so he set to work gathering the things he needed from the garage. While he was there, he came across a special face mask to keep out paint fumes.

Clearly, it wasn't meant for bears, because, although it covered the end of his nose, it was nowhere near his eyes. All the same, having slipped the elastic bands over his ears to hold it in place, he spent some time looking at his reflection in the wing mirror of Mr Brown's car and as far as he could make out all his whiskers were safely tucked away inside it.

Once in the garden he set to work with a wire brush on a rainwater pipe at the rear of the house.

'I must say he looks like some creature from outer space,' said Mrs Bird, gazing out of the kitchen window.

'At least it keeps him occupied,' said Mrs

Brown. 'I can't help being uneasy whenever he's at a loose end.'

'The devil finds work for idle paws,' agreed Mrs Bird, almost immediately wishing she hadn't said it in case she was tempting fate.

But much to everyone's surprise Paddington made such a good job of the first pipes, even Mrs Bird's eagle eyes couldn't find anything amiss when she inspected them. There wasn't a single spot of paint to be seen anywhere on the surrounding brickwork.

And even if it meant she would never be able to use her plastic gloves or her apron again she didn't have the heart to complain. It was a small price to pay for having number thirty-two Windsor Gardens made secure, *and* keeping Paddington occupied into the bargain.

'What did I tell you, Mary?' said Mr Brown,

looking up from his morning paper when she passed on the news.

'I only hope he doesn't try shinning up the pipes to see if it works,' said Mrs Brown. 'You know how keen he is on testing things.'

'It's a bit like giving someone a hot plate and telling them not to touch it,' agreed Mrs Bird.

As it happened, similar thoughts had been going through Paddington's mind most of the morning. At one point when he stopped for a rest he even toyed with the idea of hiding round a corner in the hope that Gentleman Dan might turn up, but with only one more drainpipe to go he decided he'd better finish off the work as quickly as possible.

It was the one just outside the landing window at the side of the house, which had been the cause of all the trouble in the first place, and he had left it until last because he wanted to make an especially good job of it for Mrs Bird's sake.

Having scrubbed the bottom section of the pipe clean with the wire brush, he mounted the steps and began work on the actual painting.

He hadn't been doing it for very long before he heard a familiar voice.

'What are you doing, bear?' barked Mr Curry.

Paddington nearly fell off the steps with alarm. The last person he wanted to see was the Browns' next-door neighbour.

'I'm painting Mr Brown's drainpipes,' he announced, regaining his balance.

'I can see that,' growled Mr Curry

suspiciously. 'The thing is, bear, why are you doing it?'

'It's some special paint which never dries,' said Paddington. 'It's very good value.'

'Paint which never dries?' repeated the Browns' neighbour. 'It doesn't sound very good value to me.'

'It was recommended to Mr Brown by a policeman,' said Paddington importantly. 'I've nearly finished all the pipes and I haven't used half the tin yet.

'Mrs Bird saw a face at the window when she came home from her shopping the other day,' he explained, seeing the sceptical look on Mr Curry's face.

'The policeman thought it might have been someone called "Gentleman Dan, the Drainpipe Man" who climbed up this very pipe. Mrs Bird said it gave her quite a turn. She hasn't got over it yet.'

'I'm not surprised,' said Mr Curry. 'Let's hope they catch him.'

'I don't think he'll be back,' said Paddington. 'Not if he saw Mrs Bird on the warpath, but Mr Brown thinks it's better to be safe than sorry.'

'Hmm,' said Mr Curry. 'What did you say it's called, bear?'

'Miracle non-dry paint for outside use,' said Paddington, reading from the can. He held it up for Mr Curry to see. 'You can buy it at any good do-it-yourself shop.'

'I don't want to do-it-myself, bear!' growled Mr Curry. 'I have more important things to do. Besides, I'm on my way out.'

He paused for a moment. 'On the other hand, I would be more than interested in having my own pipes done. I do have some very valuable items about the house. Family heirlooms, you know.'

'Have you really?' said Paddington with interest. 'I don't think I've ever seen an heirloom before.'

'And you're not starting with mine,' said the Browns' neighbour shortly.

'I don't have them on display for every Tom, Dick and bear to see. I keep them tucked away – out of the sight of prying eyes.'

Paddington couldn't help thinking if that were the case there was no point in the Browns' neighbour having his drainpipes painted, but Mr Curry was notorious for being unable to resist getting something for nothing, even if it was something he didn't need.

A cunning look came over his face. 'Did

you say you have over half a tin of paint left?' he asked.

'Nearly,' said Paddington. He was beginning to wish he hadn't mentioned it in the first place.

Mr Curry felt in his trouser pocket. 'Perhaps you would like to have a go at my pipes while you're at it,' he said. 'I'm afraid I don't have very much change on me, but I could stretch to ten pence if you do a good job.'

Paddington did a quick count-up on his paws. 'Ten pence!' he exclaimed. 'That's less than tuppence a pipe!'

'It's a well-known fact in business,' said Mr Curry, 'that the bigger the quantity, the less you pay for each individual item. It's what's known as giving discount.'

'In that case,' said Paddington hopefully,

'perhaps I could do one of your pipes for five pence?'

'Ten pence for the lot,' said Mr Curry firmly. 'That's my final offer. There's no point in having only one done.'

'I think I'd better ask Mr Brown if he minds first,' said Paddington, clutching at straws. 'It is his paint.'

'Now you don't want to do that, bear,' said Mr Curry, hastily changing his tune. 'Let it be between ourselves.'

Reaching into his pocket again, he lowered his voice. 'As I say, I have to go out now and I probably won't be back until this evening, so that will give you plenty of time to get it done. But, if you make a really good job of it, I may give you a little extra. Here's something to be going on with.'

Before Paddington had a chance to answer, something landed with a *plop* on the gravel at the foot of his steps.

Climbing down, he picked up the object and gazed at it for a moment or two before glancing up at Mr Curry's house. Unlike the Browns' drainpipes, they looked as though they hadn't seen a paintbrush in years. His heart sank as he turned the coin over in his paw. For a start it didn't even look English. In fact, the more he thought about it the less exciting Mr Curry's offer seemed, particularly when it meant doing something he hadn't bargained on in the first place.

While Paddington was considering the matter, he heard Mr Curry's front door slam shut. It was followed almost immediately afterwards by a clang from the front gate, and that, in turn, triggered off one of his brainwaves.

Shortly afterwards Paddington was hard at work again, and this time, knowing how cross the Browns would be on his behalf were they able to see what he was doing, he intended getting it over and done with as quickly as possible.

Later that day the Browns were in the middle of their afternoon tea when the peace was shattered by the sound of a violent commotion in the road outside their house.

At one point Mrs Bird thought she heard loud cries of 'Bear', and shortly afterwards there was the sound of a police siren, but by the time she got to the front window all was quiet.

They had hardly settled down again before there was a ring at the front doorbell.

'I'll go this time, Mrs Bird!' said Paddington eagerly, and before the others could stop him he was on his way.

When he returned, he was accompanied by the policeman who had visited them earlier in the week.

'Will someone please tell me what's going on?' said Mr Brown.

'Allow me,' said the officer before Paddington had a chance to open his mouth.

He produced his notebook. 'First of all, a short while ago we received a call from one of your neighbours reporting a disturbance outside number thirty-three. We arrived at the scene as quickly as we could. The gate was wide open and a gentleman covered in black paint was dancing about in the gutter, shouting his head off. Assuming it must be Gentleman Dan, the Drainpipe Man, we placed him under immediate arrest.

'On our way back to the station, we managed to quieten him down . . .' the policeman looked up from his notebook, 'which was no easy task, I can tell you. He informed us he was your next-door neighbour, so we removed the handcuffs and brought him back. I dare say you will be able to confirm you have a Mr Curry living next door.'

'I'm afraid we do,' said Mrs Brown.

'What did he look like?' asked Mr Brown.

'Well, he's not exactly a bear lover for a start,' said the policeman. 'Kept going on about the iniquities of someone called Paddington . . .'

'Say no more,' broke in Mrs Bird. 'That's him.'

'Well,' continued the officer, 'when we arrived back at his house, who should we meet coming out of the gate, but none other than Gentleman Dan, the Drainpipe Man. He must have seen us drive off and seized his chance.

'He had the cheek to say he'd gone to the wrong door by mistake.'

'Did he get away with much?' asked Mr Brown.

'Didn't have a thing on him,' said the officer, 'which is a pity, because I gather from Mr Curry that he has a lot of valuable items, and we could have booked him on the spot.

'On the other hand, I don't think he'll be bothering us again for a while. Thanks to this young bear's efforts, we've not only got a picture of him, but we have his "dabs" for good measure.'

He turned to Paddington. 'I'd like to shake you by the paw for your sterling work,' he said.

Paddington eyed the policeman's hand doubtfully. There was a large lump of something black attached to the palm.

'Perhaps you would like to borrow some of Mr Brown's white spirit first,' he said. 'You won't want to get any of that on your steering wheel.'

'You've got a point,' said the policeman, taking a look at it himself. 'Seeing as how I recommended it in the first place, I can't really complain, but . . .'

'I still don't quite understand,' said Mr Brown, after the officer had left. 'What's all this about painting Mr Curry's front gate?'

Paddington took a deep breath. 'I thought if I stopped any burglars getting into his garden in the first place, they wouldn't be able to break into his house, and it would save using up all your paint on his downpipes. I forgot Mr Curry still had to get back in!'

The Browns fell silent as they digested this latest piece of information.

'It seemed like a good idea at the time,' said Paddington lamely.

'You can't really blame Paddington, Henry,' said Mrs Brown. 'You did take him up on his offer after all.'

'How much was Mr Curry going to pay you for doing his pipes?' asked Mr Brown.

'Ten pence,' said Paddington.

'In that case,' said Mrs Bird, amid general

agreement, 'I have no sympathy. That man deserves all he gets. *And* he knows it.

'If he says anything to you about it,' she added grimly, turning to Paddington, 'tell him to come and see me first.'

'Thank you very much, Mrs Bird,' said Paddington gratefully. 'If you like, I'll go round and tell him now.'

The Browns exchanged glances. 'It's very kind of you, Paddington,' said Mrs Brown. 'But you've had a very busy day, and I do think it's a case of "least said, soonest mended". Why don't you put your paws up for a while?'

Having considered the matter, Paddington thought it was a very good idea indeed. And, funnily enough, Mr Curry never did mention the day he *didn't* get his drainpipes painted, although for some weeks to come, whenever Paddington waved to the Browns' neighbour over the garden fence he received some very black looks in return.

They were even darker than the colour of his front gate, which now remained permanently open.

On the other hand, Mrs Bird never again saw a face looking at her through the landing window.

The Wishing Fish Clock

Joyce Dunbar
Illustrated by Yabaewah Scott

In the town of Cheltenham there is a shopping arcade.

In the shopping arcade there is a clock.

It is called the 'Wishing Fish Clock'.

At the top of the clock there is a white duck that lays golden eggs.

At the bottom of the clock, like a pendulum, there is a great wooden fish with a wide open mouth. This fish is as big as a boat. Every hour, on the hour, he plays a tune – 'I'm For Ever Blowing Bubbles'. His eyes switch on and off, his fins flip to and fro, and bubbles pour out of his mouth.

There is a mouse that goes in and out of doors at the sides of the clock, and a snake that tries to eat the mouse. The snake would like to steal the golden eggs. The snake never gets the mouse, and he never gets near the golden eggs.

This makes him feel very spiteful!

He is a spiteful yellow and green, with a wicked forked tongue and red eyes. But the mouse doesn't know he is there and the duck isn't worried about her eggs.

A brass sun on the big hand of the clock smiles all the time at passers-by. The minute hand is a crescent moon. The clock hangs high up on the wall, way above people's heads. But they always stop to stare at the clock, and when they see the mouse that goes in and out, and the duck that lays golden eggs, their faces light up and they smile. They forget about their shopping for a while and remember something long lost.

As for the children – every hour, near the hour, they gather under the clock. They count the seconds ticking by. There! It's four o'clock! The clock face goes into a spin, with painted animals chasing each other. The fish plays his tune and blows his bubbles. Then, laughing and clapping and leaping in the air, the children catch every one. For each bubble they can burst they get a wish.

The duck and the fish and the mouse love the shopping arcade. They love it by day when the sun gilds the great glass-domed roof and they love it when the moon makes it silver. The snake likes it best in the dark. Then he tries harder than ever to eat the mouse and steal the golden eggs.

The duck and the fish and the mouse love watching the people down below.

'See how their faces light up!' says the duck.

'Look how they smile!' says the fish.

'Aren't people—' says the mouse, popping out, but he can never finish his sentence because he has to go in again, '*wonderful!*' he says, inside the clock.

But the snake looks sly and stays silent. He is waiting for his chance.

One evening, when there was neither sun

nor moon and all the shoppers had gone home, a different sort of person came along.

He didn't look up at the clock but kept his gaze fixed on the ground. He didn't look into the shop windows, but kept his hands deep in his pockets. At eight o'clock, when the painted animals started chasing each other and the fish played his tune and blew his bubbles, he did not smile at all.

This person was a tramp. He had no home to go to, no bed to sleep in and no food to eat.

'Why are you so unhappy?' said the fish, with a mouth full of bubbles.

'I think it's because of the world,' said the tramp.

'What's wrong with the world?' asked the fish.

'That,' said the tramp, 'would be telling.'

'I thought *this* was the world,' said the duck.

'Well, it isn't,' said the tramp. 'This is a shopping arcade. The world is all outside.'

'Aren't people—' said the mouse, popping out, *'wonderful!'* he said, popping in.

The tramp just shrugged his shoulders.

'Tell us about the world,' said the fish.

'It is not what it seems,' said the tramp.

'I *know!*' hissed the snake.

'What do you *mean*?' asked the fish.

'Aren't people—' said the mouse, popping out of the door near the snake, *'wonderful!'* he said, popping in.

The snake hissed, snatched and missed.

'People are not what they seem,' said the tramp.

'I *know*!' hissed the snake.

'What do you *mean*?' asked the fish.

The tramp looked thoughtful for a moment. 'Out there in the world,' he began, 'there are other creatures like you – marvellous creatures called whales. They don't hang on a wall. They swim in the wide vast oceans. They sing songs that echo in the deeps. Great water spouts gush from their heads. These creatures are in danger—'

'Danger?' said the fish.

'They are in danger from people!' said the tramp.

'Are there other creatures like me?' said the duck.

'Ah,' said the tramp, shaking his head, 'there are other creatures like you – magnificent creatures called eagles. They don't sit on top of a clock. They soar in the highest skies. They are not tame like you, but fierce and wild and free. These creatures are in danger—'

'Danger?' said the duck.

'People steal their eggs,' said the tramp.

'How?' hissed the snake.

'Are there other creatures—' said the mouse, popping out, 'like me?' he said, popping in.

'Yes, there are!' shouted the tramp, so that he could be heard inside the clock. 'Millions of creatures like you, and some that are very much bigger. Enormous gigantic elephants! They do not live in a clock. They live in the thickest jungle. The elephants are also in danger.'

'Are we in danger too?' asked the mouse, staying out longer than usual.

The snake hissed, snatched and missed.

'Perhaps not,' said the tramp.

'You must bring all the whales to see me!' said the fish.

'And all the eagles to see me!' said the duck.

'And the elephants—' said the mouse, popping out, 'to see me,' he said, popping in.

'We will warn them!' said the fish.

'You don't understand!' said the tramp. 'One single whale would fill the whole of the shopping arcade. An elephant would go thundering through it. He might smash all the shop windows! And the eagle—'

'What would the eagle do?' asked the duck.

'The eagle might eat that snake,' said the tramp.

'You must bring them just the same!' said the fish, the mouse and the duck.

'You don't understand!' said the tramp. 'The whales need the sea! The eagles need the sky! The elephants need the jungle!'

'Then you must bring the sea to see me,' said the fish, 'and I will teach it to blow bubbles.'

'And you must bring the sky to see me,' said the duck, 'and I will teach it to lay eggs!'

'And you must bring the jungle to see me,' said the mouse, managing to stay out all the while, 'and I will teach it to go in and out!'

'The sea blowing bubbles! The sky laying eggs! The jungle going in and out!' said the tramp, hopping from one leg to the other with the difficulty of it all. 'That's not the answer to anything! That wouldn't solve a single thing! It's *people* that cause all the trouble! It's *people* you need to teach! And *people* will never learn!'

'I *know!*' hissed the snake.

'What about the children?' asked the fish.

'Children are all very well,' said the tramp, 'but they mostly grow up to be *people!*'

The tramp was getting really worked up. He paced up and down the arcade, his voice getting louder and louder.

'*People* are a very great *puzzle! Somebody* should do *something* about it!'

'Aren't you a people?' said the fish.

'I am,' said the tramp.

'And is what you say quite true?' said the duck.

'It is,' said the tramp.

'And is there nothing—' said the mouse, popping out, 'we can do?' he said, popping in.

'Nothing,' said the tramp.

'Can't you wish?' said the fish.

'Wishes won't help,' said the tramp.

'Then I will stop blowing bubbles,' said the fish.

'And I will stop laying eggs,' said the duck.

'And I will stop going in and out,' said the mouse.

And the mouse stayed out, right under the eyes of the snake, right under his spiteful forked tongue. The mouse stayed there, very very still. Close by him was a golden egg.

The snake arched his long thin neck. He hissed his terrible hiss. He stretched out his deadly tongue. He was poised, ready to strike!

But suddenly, the whole clock stopped.

The snake was forced to stop too. Oh, what spite in his eyes! And oh, what fear in the mouse!

The tramp was completely dumbfounded. He didn't know what to do.

'No, no, it's not true . . .' he began saying to the clock.

'Come on now, move along there. You know you're not allowed to sleep in here,' said another voice.

It was a policeman, talking to the tramp.

'But the clock!' said the tramp.

'What about the clock?' said the policeman.

'It's stopped!' said the tramp.

'Well, there's not much you can do about it,' said the policeman.

'You don't understand,' said the tramp. 'It's my fault the clock has stopped! I have made it despair!'

'Move along there,' said the policeman, and he began pushing the tramp out of the arcade, out into the cold dark night, where there was neither sun nor moon.

'It's not true!' yelled out the tramp. 'It's not true what I said about the world! It's a story! I made it all up! The world is a shopping arcade! What you do is very important! What you do makes people happy! The children! Think of the children! It was a people who made you anyway!'

The next morning, very early, a man came along to look at the clock. He opened a door at the back and tinkered with some machinery inside. Soon the duck started laying eggs again. The mouse went in and out. The snake hissed, snatched and missed.

At eight o'clock, on the hour, the fish began to blow bubbles.

'It was a people who made us!' he said.

'And a people who got us going again!' said the duck.

'Aren't people—' said the mouse, popping out, '*wonderful*!' he said, inside the clock.

'I *don't know*!' hissed the snake. 'I don't know!'

Tea at Mrs Manderby's

Adèle Geras
Illustrated by Penny Bell

'...**T**wenty-two, twenty-three, twenty-four, twenty-five. There!' Hannah smiled at the pennies she'd been counting: this week's pocket money, and a few pennies from last week's, and the rest from the transparent plastic pig in which she kept her savings. She pushed them in a long line across the table, and then began to pile them into shaky brown towers.

'Let's go to the shop now, Dad,' she said, but Dad was washing plates noisily in the sink, and not paying attention. 'Dad?'

'What?'

'I said, may we go to the shop now?'

'Which shop is that?'

'The junk shop,' said Hannah.

'What for?'

'To buy something.'

'I don't know what Mum'll say. We've got a whole house full of junk, quite a lot of it in your room, too. Why do you want to spend good pocket money on it?'

'It's not junk I want to buy. It's a doll. I saw it there last week.'

'It's probably been sold, then,' said Dad, swooshing fluffy soapsuds down into the plughole with his hands.

'No it hasn't.' Hannah smiled.

'How do you know?'

'Because I asked Mr Spatten to keep it for me, and he said he would, if I paid him some money as a deposit. He explained all about it. You pay some money, and it means that something is a bit yours, but not enough to take away. Then you go and pay the rest of the money, and after that what you want is all yours and you can take it home.'

'Where did you get the money from?' Dad asked.

'I saved it.'

'I see. Well, all right then, if you let me drink my coffee in peace, and give me half an hour to read the paper, then we'll go down to the junk shop together. Okay?'

'Okay,' said Hannah. 'There are things I have to do, anyway.'

Dad was already reading. From time to time, his hand crept out round the side of the newspaper, and waved over the table, like a slow, five-headed creature with bad eyesight, looking for the cup. Hannah put the money into her pencil case and went upstairs.

In her room, she dropped each penny carefully into her purse, and then she put the purse into her best red handbag. 'You lot,' she said to the row of plump, well-dressed dolls lined up on the shelf, 'are going to have a big surprise today.' Hannah waited for the dolls to take in this news, and then went on: 'Yes,

I'm bringing home a friend for you, and you are all to be nice to her. I won't have any rude remarks about how shabby she is, and you're to have her to all your tea parties.' Ruby Tuesday, the brown velvet rag doll, had a doubtful look in her eye. 'Ruby,' said Hannah, 'she's really lovely. She was in a big box when I found her. How would you like to lie in a cardboard box full of broken saucers, and cracked photograph frames, and old plastic egg cups and dirty shoes? I had to rescue her, didn't I?' Dolly Daydream's pink, turned-up nose turned up even higher, it seemed to Hannah. 'Dolly,' she said, 'I shall clean her up, don't you worry, and then I dare say she'll be as pretty as you. Prettier, even.' All the dolls made round eyes, full of amazement. Dolly Daydream was the most expensive of them all, and the biggest. Hannah thought she was stuck up and not a bit cuddly, with cold, pink hands and feet and fat, smug cheeks. 'Jenny, you'll look after her, I know, because you're so kind.' Jenny had been loved to tatters since Hannah was a baby, but her bright red smile was still neatly stitched to her cotton face, and what was left of her brown wool hair was tidily parted in the middle. 'What shall we call her?' Hannah asked the dolls. Ruby, Dolly Daydream, Jenny, Little Sadie, Skinny Lizzy and all the others said nothing. Hannah said: 'Well, you're a lot of help, I must say. I shall think of a name all by myself.' She thought for a moment. 'The new doll will be called Belle. I've just decided.' This was not quite true. Belle had been the name of the doll in the junk shop for a whole week, ever since

Hannah had pulled her out of the rubbish box. It suited her perfectly.

'Hannah!' shouted Dad from downstairs, 'are you coming, then? We have to be back before Mum gets home from the library. We're going to tea at Mrs Manderby's, remember?'

'Coming, Dad,' said Hannah, and felt herself turning cross and sad all over. Why did today, her special, Belle-buying day, have to be spoiled by tea at Mrs Manderby's? Hannah could never understand why they had to go. On the way to the shop, she asked: 'Why do we go there? I hate her.'

'Don't say that, Hannah. It's not kind and it's not true. Mrs Manderby is a lonely old lady, who doesn't have a great deal of fun in her life. She looks forward to seeing us. It's a treat for her.'

'Then why is she so cross? Why does she never smile? Why do I have to sit still and keep quiet? Why can't I touch things in her house? Why is it so dark and stuffy in her lounge? Why doesn't she let me have more than two biscuits? Why can't I go there in my jeans?'

'Gosh!' said Dad. 'Is this some kind of quiz show? I've never heard so many questions in all my life. One answer for all of them, really.'

'What is it?'

'When Mrs Manderby was a girl, the world was very different. No television, very few cars or aeroplanes. People had different ideas then about how children should behave and dress, and Mrs Manderby is simply treating you in the way that she was treated when she was a child.'

'I don't believe she ever was a child,' said Hannah.

'Of course she was, love. Everyone was a child once.'

'But she's so thin and pointed and black and straight, I just can't see her as a child. I think she was always just like she is now.'

'Come on,' said Dad. 'Forget about Mrs Manderby for a while and let's go and fetch that doll.'

Hannah and her father went into the junk shop, and Hannah wondered for the hundredth time why the treasures that stood heaped on shelves and in boxes and on the floor were called 'junk'. Who had decided that a plate with a picture of floating blue ribbons and pink roses should be thrown out? Why did the owner of the china cups with dragons curling round the edges not like them enough to keep them? Didn't people collect postcards any more? There were boxes of old, brown, picture postcards with spidery, forgotten handwriting on the back – did nobody want to remember holidays and journeys? Hannah loved everything in the shop, everything that was no more use to anyone.

'I'm going to see what I can find,' said Dad. He enjoyed the junk shop as much as Hannah, although his treasures were of a different kind: records with torn covers, books with gold writing on the spine, and little, black letters squeezed together into lines. Hannah went up to Mr Spatten, who was standing behind a counter full of old lamps, candlesticks and mountains of white plates.

'Good afternoon, Mr Spatten,' she said politely.

'Ah,' said Mr Spatten, pushing his glasses into a better position on his nose, and wiping his feathery moustache with a spotted handkerchief. 'Miss Hannah, is it? Yes? Are you well? Are you happy? Do you see anything your heart desires or your house requires?'

'I can't see it, Mr Spatten, what my heart desires, I mean, but I know you've kept it for me.' Mr Spatten looked puzzled. 'The doll,' Hannah said quickly. 'You said you'd keep her for me. I found her in that box over there. I paid you a deposit of one penny. You said you'd keep her for me.'

'Ah . . . a deposit, now, is it? Bless my little cotton socks, you're going to be a banker when you grow up. Who told you about deposits?'

'You did, Mr Spatten.' Hannah's voice remained polite, but her heart was bumping about so loudly that she could hear it in her head. Had Mr Spatten forgotten? Had he sold the doll? Hannah gulped. 'You put her into a drawer. You promised to look after her.'

'I'm sure you're right, child. Let's have a shufti.'

'What's that? I don't want a shufti. I want my doll.' Tears were winking in Hannah's eyes, fighting to come out. She blinked them away.

Mr Spatten said: 'A shufti means a look. Let's have a look is what I meant. This one first, I think.' He picked at things in a jumbled drawer, and said 'Amazing what you find, isn't it? When you visit a drawer after a long time.

Only a messy one, mind. No adventures in a tidy drawer, are there?'

He found the doll at last, half-hidden under a felt hat with holes in the brim. 'There she is!' shouted Hannah. 'There's Belle!'

'Aha! I see now why you were so anxious to find her,' said Mr Spatten. 'In bad condition, and no clothes to speak of, but yes, a beauty. A china-headed doll, with a stuffed leather body, dating from about 1900. An old doll indeed. And how much am I charging for this treasure?'

'You said 25p,' said Hannah, taking out her purse.

'I'm a fool,' said Mr Spatten, 'but there you are. I think I shall put the price up . . .' (a tear plopped from Hannah's eye and puddled on to the dusty glass of the counter)

'. . . to 25p and a big, happy smile from you, my girl.'

'Oh, thank you,' said Hannah, and smiled till her cheeks hurt. She poured the twenty-five pence on to the counter and took Belle into her arms. 'There's one back for you, you know,' said Mr Spatten. 'Don't forget you've already paid one penny as a deposit.' Hannah took it.

'Goodbye, Mr Spatten,' she said. 'Thank you so much.'

When Hannah and her father arrived home, Mum was waiting. She worked as a librarian, and always finished early on Saturdays. After she had admired Belle for five whole minutes, she sent Hannah upstairs to change into a dress. The time had come for tea at Mrs Manderby's. Hannah said to Belle: 'You can come too, Belle. I won't mind so much if you're there. I shall sit on my chair and hold you on my lap. I don't care how sour Mrs Manderby looks, I shall talk to you, that's all.'

The Blaines's house and Mrs Manderby's house were in the same street, and it took exactly sixty seconds to cross the road and travel back in time over fifty years. The strangeness began in the garden. Every other garden in the street had roses in the summer, daffodils and crocuses clumped together in the spring, and rhododendrons that looked good enough to eat: sugar pink, and pale mauve and white. Some hedges were neat, others untidy. Some drives were swept clean, others were dotted with leaves, crisp bags, and old notes written to the milkman. But in

Mrs Manderby's garden flowers did what they were told, and lived in round, neatly made beds cut into the grass. The lawn always looked as if it had just been brushed and combed. Not a single leaf stuck out from the flat surface of the hedge, and there was not a crisp bag in the whole world brave enough to blow on to Mrs Manderby's drive.

Dad knocked at the door, and Hannah heard the tapping of the old lady's stick on the wooden floor. The first thing, thought Hannah, was to get safely past the tiger skin stretched out in the hall. It was only the skin of a tiger, but Hannah didn't like the way the head stuck up, and she hated the amber glass eyes and the yellowing teeth. She clutched Belle under one arm, and hung on to her mother's hand.

'My dears.' Mrs Manderby had opened the

door. 'How very kind of you to call. Do come in. How do you do, Hannah?'

'How do you do, Mrs Manderby?' Hannah answered politely. The first time Mrs Manderby had asked her how she did, Hannah had said: 'I'm fine, thank you,' and Mrs Manderby had spent the rest of the afternoon talking about the absence of good manners in the world today. It still seemed silly to Hannah to answer one question with another, and she thought that people only did it when they couldn't think of anything interesting to talk about.

Dad held the door open while the ladies (which included Hannah) followed Mrs Manderby into the room which Hannah called the lounge, and Mrs Manderby called the drawing room. Hannah sat on the chair with a tapestry seat which made her legs itch. If only she could have worn her jeans. Dad and Mum sat on a funny kind of sofa with no arms and only half a back, which was called a *chaise longue*. This, Hannah had been told, meant 'long chair' in French. Mrs Manderby sat in a brown leather chair with fat armrests. The room looked dark, even though the sun was shining. Maybe it was the maroon wallpaper and the almost-black wood of the table. Hannah shut her ears to the quiet talk of the grown-ups and chatted to Belle in her head: *Isn't it awful, not being able to touch? Look at that box. I bet it's a musical box. Can you see the apple tree in the back garden? Maybe I'll ask to go out after tea. Mrs Manderby's husband shot the tiger in India, a long time ago. That's him over there. Doesn't he look funny in that hat? Mrs*

*Manderby hasn't any children. I wonder
what she does when we're not here? I wonder
what upstairs is like . . . ?* Mrs Manderby's
voice pulled Hannah out of her thoughts.

'. . . Like a biscuit, my dear?'

'Yes, please,' said Hannah, and stood up
to take one. As she did so, Belle fell off her
lap and flopped on to the carpet, taking with
her the teacup that had been balanced on a
little table next to Hannah's chair. A brown
stain crept and spread over the carpet.
Hannah looked at her parents, and trembled.
Dad said: 'Never mind, love,' Mum said:
'Don't worry, I'll get a cloth,' and Hannah
said: 'I'm terribly sorry,' all at the same time.
They all waited for Mrs Manderby's anger.
But Mrs Manderby wasn't listening. She had
picked Belle up, and was sitting with the old

doll in her lap, turning her over and over, fingering the torn lace of her dress, and stroking her smooth, hard cheek. Mrs Manderby's eyes shone with tears as she stared at Belle. She took a handkerchief out of her pocket and wiped them. Hannah could not understand why the old lady was so upset. She prayed for an earthquake or a flood: something that would make Mrs Manderby forget about the carpet. It was an accident. Everyone spilled cups of things by mistake. She thought of her father's hand, waving above the coffee cup at lunchtime. Why, then, was Mrs Manderby crying? Hannah supposed she must love the carpet. She said: 'Don't worry, Mrs Manderby. We can send the carpet to the cleaners. It'll come back good as new, really. I'm ever so sorry.' Mrs

Manderby looked up and laughed through her tears. Hannah had never seen her laugh before.

'Silly goose! Do you think I'm crying about a carpet? Why, I spill things myself, nearly every day, although in my case the cause is arthritis in my fingers.'

'Then why are you crying?'

'Because I've just seen someone I loved very much a long time ago, and she hasn't changed, and I have, and it makes me feel sad.'

'There's no one here except us,' said Hannah.

'There's Clara,' said Mrs Manderby.

'Who's she?'

'The doll,' said Mrs Manderby, and held Belle's face next to her cheek.

'She's mine,' said Hannah. 'I bought her today in the junk shop.'

'And I'm glad you did. I gave her away to my godchild fifty years ago, when we left for India, and I haven't seen her since then. My lovely Clara, how battered and how miserable you look, but how beautiful, still.' Mrs Manderby handed the doll back to Hannah. 'I'm sure you will take care of her, and never give her away.'

'I won't,' said Hannah, 'not even if I go to India when I'm grown-up.'

'Perhaps we could make her a new dress.' The old lady's eyes shone. 'You must come tomorrow, Hannah, and help me sort out the trunks upstairs. All my old evening gowns are there, and my fans. We could make her a few very pretty frocks. Would you like that?'

'I'd love it. I'll come tomorrow. Would you like to see my other dolls?'

'Certainly. We'll have a tea party under the apple tree. All your dolls are cordially invited.'

Hannah grinned. 'They all cordially accept,' she said.

It was time to go home. As they stood at the door, Hannah saw her father and Mrs Manderby whispering together. Then he bounded up the stairs and came down holding an old photograph with curled-over edges. He gave it to Hannah. Mrs Manderby said: 'That's me, aged five. And that's Clara.'

Hannah looked. A fat little girl, dressed in a frilly white pinafore and high-buttoned boots, stared at her from under a curly fringe of black hair. In her hand was Belle, dressed in lace and ribbons. Hannah put the photograph into Mrs Manderby's hand. She said: 'You're both the same now, really, only older. I shall call Belle Clarabelle, because she *is* yours, still, as well as mine. Is Clarabelle a good name?'

'An excellent name,' said Mrs Manderby. 'Very elegant and genteel.'

Hannah said: 'See you tomorrow', and followed her mother and father down the drive.

The next day, at four o'clock, Hannah and Mrs Manderby sat under the apple tree together. The dolls, all dressed for the party, were lined up on the grass beside a white tablecloth embroidered with flowers and trailing leaves. Clarabelle wore a long blue taffeta skirt made out of an old scarf that Mrs Manderby had found, and she had a square of lace fastened round her shoulders like a shawl.

'I had a beautiful doll's tea set when I was a girl,' said Mrs Manderby. 'I wonder what became of it. It would have been such fun to set it out for the dolls this afternoon.'

'Never mind,' said Hannah. 'I think these are lovely.' She put a cup and saucer in front of each of the dolls. 'They've never had such a grand tea before. Neither have I. Gold-rimmed cups!'

Mrs Manderby had bought cream cakes. There was a plate piled with sandwiches and decorated with frilly lettuce leaves. There were scones with strawberry jam and cream. Mrs Manderby poured tea from a silver teapot with a long curved spout. 'Do eat as much as you can, dear,' she said.

Hannah did. She ate for herself and for all the dolls. They just sat and smiled in the sunshine that fell through the leaves of the apple tree and made gold spots of light on their pretty dresses.

Macaw and the Blackberry Fishcakes

John Escott
Illustrated by Yabaewah Scott

When Patsy's mum and dad took over Crab Cove's fish and chip shop, they took over Macaw as well.

Patsy, who had always wanted a pet bird, thought Macaw was beautiful with his red, yellow and blue wings and his red breast. Unfortunately, her mother did not think Macaw was quite so lovely.

'I'd have thought twice about coming if I'd known that bird was here,' Mrs Forum said. 'I'm sure it will cost us a fortune to keep.'

Macaw had been left behind by the old owner of the shop because he was going into a rest home and couldn't take his bird with him. Rest homes had strict rules about such things.

'Isn't there a tropical bird garden we can give him to?' Mrs Forum wondered.

'Squam!' screamed Macaw.

'I don't think he likes that idea,' Mr Forum told his wife.

'Nor do I,' said Patsy, pulling a face.

So Macaw stayed, which pleased Patsy very much. And things went quite smoothly until the day of the Crab Cove Hospital Fête . . .

The fête began in the morning and went on all day. Patsy's mum was helping out on Mrs Hatwhistle's stall. Patsy and Macaw had gone along as well.

Macaw was perched in his favourite spot on Patsy's mop of red hair. 'yark!' he shrieked at passers-by, but in a friendly way.

Mrs Hatwhistle's stall was full of goodies. Home-made wine, home-made jam, cakes, biscuits.

'Everything looks lovely, Mrs Hatwhistle,' said Patsy.

'Hatwhistle!' screamed Macaw.

'Really, Patsy!' said Mrs Forum, looking

embarrassed. 'You must teach that bird some manners.'

'Sorry, Mrs Hatwhistle,' said Patsy.

'Bless me, dear, I don't mind,' laughed Mrs Hatwhistle. 'I think Macaw is a scream.'

'Scream!' screamed Macaw.

'Er – we'll have a look round and come back later,' said Patsy.

Now at this time, out in the middle of Crab Bay, there was a large white luxury yacht. It belonged to Mr Hiram J. Beefy, the American beefburger millionaire. He owned burger bars all over America and was shaped a bit like a beefburger himself.

Mr Beefy and his wife, Lydia, were on a world cruise.

'What a darling little place,' Mrs Beefy said

when she saw Crab Cove. She was as thin as a stick insect, which made people laugh when they heard her married name.

Hiram J. sighed. 'Yes, honey.' He was bored with cruising. Getting ideas to improve his burger bars was what interested him, and he didn't think Crab Cove would provide him with any of those.

But he was wrong.

Back at the fête, Macaw had taken off from Patsy's hair (which he had got into the habit of using as a landing pad) and flown over to Mrs Hatwhistle's stall again. He seemed especially interested in a bottle of wine that hung in a basket under the canopy of the stall.

'Blackberry Wine – only £1.50' it said on the label.

'Squaw!' said Macaw – and he picked up the basket by the handle and flew off with it, over the heads of the crowd.

'Macaw!' cried Mrs Forum. 'Bring that back at once.'

Macaw didn't even look round.

A few minutes later, when Patsy arrived back carrying a large chocolate ice cream, she could see something was wrong by the look on her mother's face.

'Where's Macaw?' she said.

'That *bird*!' shouted Mrs Forum.

In fact, Macaw had taken his prize home. He flew into the kitchen at the back of Forum's Fish Parlour and perched on a shelf above the worktop.

Then, slowly, he pecked the cork from the

bottle of wine, the neck hanging over the edge of the shelf . . .

. . . And the wine poured steadily downwards – straight into a large bowl which stood on the worktop. In the bowl was a fishy mixture.

Macaw lost interest in the bottle after the wine had stopped gurgling and he flew out of the window in search of some new adventure.

The fishy mixture gradually changed colour.

Several minutes later, Mr Forum returned to his kitchen after answering the phone. 'Now what was I doing?' he said to himself. 'Ah, yes. The fishcake mix.' And he went over to the large bowl on the worktop and began stirring it. He didn't notice that the fishcake mix had more of a pinky tinge to it now.

* * *

Out on Hiram J. Beefy's yacht, the millionaire and his wife were having a late breakfast. Mrs Beefy was eating a grapefruit, while her husband tucked into a king-sized beefburger of the sort that had made him his fortune.

Suddenly, there was a flapping sound, and they both turned to see Macaw landing on the rail of the yacht.

'Look, honey,' said Hiram J. 'It's a macaw!'

Lydia looked tickled pink. 'I wonder if it talks?' she said.

She didn't have to wonder long.

'Pie-and-chips-chicken-and-chips-pea-fritters-fishcakes-pass-the-vinegar!' screamed Macaw.

Hiram J. stared in astonishment. 'Did you hear that, Lydia? He's telling you what is on the menu at some restaurant. Now that's what I call smart. A flying advertisement!'

'Where's-the-salt?' shrieked Macaw, and flew off towards Crab Cove.

Hiram J. Beefy forgot about his breakfast. 'I have to find out where he's going. I've never tasted a pea fritter. Who knows, maybe it's something I can introduce into the Burger Bars.'

And he called for one of his crew to launch the small boat.

Patsy had arrived back at the shop in time for the midday opening. Because Mrs Forum was staying at the fête, Patsy was to act as waitress at the four tables in Forum's Fish Parlour. But she was worried about Macaw.

Patsy told her father what the bird had done at the fête.

'Dear me,' was all that Mr Forum said.

At that moment, Macaw flew past the window and perched on the hanging sign outside the shop.

'There he is!' cried Patsy.

'He's not carrying any bottles of wine,' Mr Forum observed.

'Oh dear,' said Patsy. 'I wonder what he's done with it.'

Just then, a large man in expensive yachting clothes came into the shop and collapsed into a chair at one of the tables. He had obviously been running. 'Is that . . . your bird?' he gasped, nodding to Macaw outside.

'Er – yes,' Patsy admitted, wondering what Macaw had been up to now.

But the man just gave a nod and said, 'Good'. Without looking at the menu, he said,

'I'll have two pea fritters, two fishcakes and some chips, please.'

'Yes, sir,' said Patsy, one eye on Macaw.

'Yessir!' said Macaw through the open window.

The American stayed right through lunchtime. He ate what he had ordered, then he asked Patsy to bring him some more of 'those delicious fishcakes'.

'He's got an enormous appetite,' Patsy whispered to her father.

'It's very strange,' said Mr Forum, 'but several customers have come back for more fishcakes today. They're all saying how nice they are. It's a good job I made an extra-large helping of mixture.'

It was much later, when Patsy was busy

clearing up in the kitchen, that she glanced up and saw the empty wine bottle on the shelf.

'So *that's* where it got to,' she said. Then she noticed the empty bowl on the worktop beneath it. 'Oh, my goodness. Dad!' she called.

Mr Forum came into the kitchen.

'Uh – your fishcakes,' she said. 'Did you mix them in that?' Patsy nodded to the bowl beneath the empty wine bottle.

'Yes,' said Mr Forum. 'Why?'

Patsy pointed to the empty wine bottle. 'I – er – think you had something extra in today's mix.'

Mr Forum looked up at the bottle. 'Whatever . . . ?'

'Mrs Hatwhistle's blackberry wine,' said Patsy.

'Oh!' said Mr Forum.

Later, when the shop was closing for the afternoon, Hiram J. Beefy went over to the counter to speak to Mr Forum and Patsy.

'Sir,' he said. 'I'd like to congratulate you on a most original dish.'

'You would?' said Mr Forum, looking surprised.

The American nodded. 'I'm talking about your fishcakes. I've never tasted any like them before. You must have your own special recipe.'

'Well—' began Mr Forum.

Hiram J. held up a hand. 'Now I don't expect

you to tell me your recipe for nothing. What do you say to a thousand dollars?'

Mr Forum blinked in astonishment. Patsy's mouth fell open.

'Oh – well, really – I couldn't—' Mr Forum began.

'Nonsense,' said Hiram J. 'I insist on paying you something. I want to make and sell them in my Burger Bars in America.'

'But – but it was an accident,' said Mr Forum.

Now it was Hiram J. Beefy's turn to look surprised. 'Accident?'

Mr Forum explained about Macaw and the bottle of wine. 'And so what you had this morning,' he finished, 'were *blackberry* fishcakes. A sort of *freak* fishcake.'

Hiram J. began to laugh. 'Let's get this

straight,' he chuckled. 'It's a normal fishcake mix, plus one bottle of blackberry wine?' And he laughed and laughed.

Patsy and Mr Forum laughed with him.

In the end, because Mr Forum wouldn't take any money, the millionaire made a generous donation to the hospital fête fund. And Mr Forum told him how to make pea fritters, free of charge, so Hiram J. Beefy went away a very happy man.

'Wait until we tell Mum,' said Patsy, after the American had gone. 'She'll have to let Macaw stay now. Blackberry fishcakes could make us millionaires like Mr Beefy.'

'Well, we've already sold more than three times the number we usually do,' he agreed. 'We must tell Mrs Hatwhistle. After all, it was her blackberry wine that did the trick. We'll have to go into business together. The Hatwhistle and Forum Blackberry Fishcake Company!' Mr Forum laughed.

'blackberry fishcakes!' screamed Macaw, automatically adding an extra item to his squawk-aloud menu. 'blackberry fishcakes!'

And after that day, they became a regular feature at Forum's Fish Parlour.

The Stonecutter

An Ethiopian Folk Story
Retold by Elizabeth Laird
Illustrated by Penny Bell

Once upon a time, high up in the mountains of Ethiopia, where buzzards soar about the crags by day, and hyenas roam the plains by night, there lived a poor stonecutter.

Every day, he took his hammer and his chisel, filled his goatskin with water, and set off for the quarry. Every day he listened to the monkeys squabble and chatter in the cliffs above, and watched the painted butterflies hover over the flowers beneath. Every day he toiled under the hot sun, chipping and chopping, hacking and hewing, carving out great stone blocks for the streets and palaces of the wily old Emperor's turreted city.

And then, one day, the wily old Emperor rode by.

Before him trotted a hundred horsemen, and their lion's mane headdresses fluttered in the breeze. Behind him ran a hundred foot soldiers, and the sun glinted on the polished tips of their spears. A servant held over his head an umbrella of turquoise silk to shield him from the heat, and his mule was covered with a saddlecloth of the richest, softest velvet.

'Oho,' said the stonecutter, as he bowed a deep bow to the imperial procession. 'That is the life for me. How I wish I was the wily old Emperor!'

The old wizard, who lived deep inside the mountain, heard his wish, and before he could blink his eyes, the stonecutter had been transformed into the Emperor. Dressed in the finest robes, he was riding the Emperor's own mule, with his horsemen, his foot soldiers and the servant with the turquoise umbrella all in respectful attendance.

'Oh wonderful, marvellous turn of fortune!' said the stonecutter, who was now the Emperor. 'Now I am the greatest of all, and everybody will obey me.'

For a time, the new Emperor was happy. He granted petitions, punished his enemies, fed his lions, and ate his meals in solemn state behind a curtain.

But one day, the Emperor set out on a journey. The sun rose high in the sky.

'Where is my silk turquoise umbrella?' said the Emperor. 'Servants, shade me from the sun!' But his servants had left the umbrella at home.

The Emperor shook his head.

'I am not, after all, the greatest thing in the world,' he said. 'The sun can make even kings and emperors break out in a sweat, just like an ordinary servant. How I wish I was the sun, high up in the sky!'

The old wizard, who lived deep inside the mountain, heard his wish, and before he could flick his fly-whisk, the Emperor had become the sun. Burning fiercely, he shone down on the land, and shrivelled up the grass, and dried up the streams and rivers, and made kings and emperors break out in a sweat, just like ordinary servants.

'Oh, magical, magnificent fate!' said the Emperor, who was now the sun. 'Now I am the greatest of all, and everybody will hide from me.'

For a time, the sun was happy. He baked the earth till it cracked, and made the elephants pant for thirst, and dried up the rivers until even the great Nile was no more than a trickle.

But one day, a cloud floated between the sun and the earth.

'My power has gone!' said the sun. 'I am not, after all, the greatest thing in the world.

This cloud can fill up the streams again, and give the grass new life, and protect the animals and people from my blinding rays. How I wish I was a cloud, pouring water down on the earth, and flooding all the fields, and making people and animals run for their lives!'

The old wizard, who lived deep inside the mountain, heard his wish, and before he could shoot forth another ray, the sun was transformed into a cloud. He floated high above the land, between the earth and the sun.

'Oh splendid, wondrous destiny!' said the sun, who was now a cloud. 'Now I am the greatest thing in the world and everybody will fear me.'

For a time, the cloud was happy. He poured torrents of water on to the land. Lightning flashed. The river burst its banks, and sheep, cows, donkeys and people were all washed away.

But there was one thing on earth that would not give way before the rushing water. It was a great rock, which stood firm, and the flood was forced to break into two streams to go round it.

'Oh!' said the cloud. 'I am not, after all, the greatest thing in the world. Oh, how I wish I was a rock! Then nothing on earth would have the power to move me.'

The old wizard, who lived deep inside the mountain, heard his wish, and before he could let loose another drop of water, the cloud had become the rock. He stood firm, and felt his mighty strength.

'Oh, happy, blessed day!' he said. 'Now I am

the greatest thing in the world, and everybody will respect me. I will watch the years come and go, and nothing will have the power to touch me.'

For a time, the rock was happy. He stood proud and firm, aloft above the plain, and looked down at the people who moved about far below.

But one day, the rock heard a chipping and a chopping, and he felt a hacking and a hewing that shuddered through his marble veins. A stonecutter was hitting at his very roots with his little hammer and chisel.

'Oh,' said the rock, 'I am not, after all, the greatest thing in the world. Not even I, in my great strength, can stop this busy fellow picking and pecking at my very roots. How I wish I was the stonecutter!'

The old wizard, who lived deep inside the mountain, heard his wish, and before he could send another shower of stones rattling down from his craggy heights, the rock found he had become the stonecutter again, toiling under the hot sun, chipping and chopping, hacking and hewing, to carve out great stone blocks for the streets and palaces of the Emperor's turreted city.

'There is nothing greater than man, and the work of his hands,' said the stonecutter, and he laughed long and loud.

The Little Fiddle

Eveline de Jong
Illustrated by Yabaewah Scott

A long time ago, almost a hundred years or so, many things were different from today. People wore different clothes and there were no cars in the streets. People didn't have radios to listen to, nor did they have televisions to watch. But there was one thing that was just the same as it is today – people enjoyed singing and making music, and they enjoyed listening to other people playing music.

At that time there lived a violin maker, who built and repaired violins. Most of the instruments he made were full-size violins for grown-ups to play, but sometimes he made smaller violins for children. One day a man came to the violin maker's shop and told him that he would like to buy a small violin for his daughter, Eleanor. Eleanor was six and she wanted to play the violin. Of course, she couldn't hold a big instrument, so she needed a small violin to learn on.

The violin maker set to work and made a beautiful small-size violin for Eleanor. When it was ready, Eleanor and her father came to fetch it. From then on the little fiddle belonged to Eleanor. She practised on it almost every day and soon she was able to play lovely tunes.

Sometimes, when Grandma came to visit, she and Eleanor would make music together: Eleanor on her little fiddle and Grandma on the piano. One day, Uncle Sam also brought his violin, and then all three played a trio together.

Eleanor grew taller, but of course the little fiddle could not grow with her. In two years Eleanor had become too big to play on the little fiddle. She needed a larger violin so that she could go on learning to play better.

The little fiddle was put away in its case. While it was lying there, it could hear Eleanor practising on her new violin. The little fiddle wished that soon there would be another child who would want to learn to play the violin and for whom it would be just the right size.

The little fiddle didn't have to wait long. One day, some friends came to visit Eleanor and her family. The children, Anna and Christian, were younger than Eleanor. They both liked singing and listening to music and both of them wanted to learn to play the violin. So the little fiddle moved to their house and Anna, who was the eldest, started having violin lessons.

After a while, Anna grew too tall for the little fiddle, but by then Christian was big enough to hold it, so the little fiddle stayed for some more happy years.

After that, for many, many years, the little fiddle lived with different children in a number of different families. Some children were happy to play, others were not. Some children made beautiful sounds and played lovely tunes, others did not.

Once, a boy fell down with the little fiddle and it broke. The boy's mother and father were very cross with him and told him that he should have been more careful. The little fiddle was worried that it was no longer fit to be played. The boy and his mother took the little fiddle to a violin maker, who repaired the break. The violin maker also put on a new set of strings, and then the little fiddle was all ready to be played again. All in all, through the ups and downs, the little fiddle had a happy time.

There was, however, just one trace of

unhappiness in the little fiddle's life: it sometimes felt a bit lonely. For whenever it played together with other violins, the little fiddle was always the smallest. The little fiddle felt overwhelmed by all the big instruments. Sometimes the little fiddle was not only surrounded by big violins, but also by large voilas, enormous cellos and even a gigantic double bass.

The little fiddle moved house again. This time it went to Vincent. Vincent liked playing the violin, but he didn't like practising. One day the little fiddle was put away in its case, and it was not taken out the following day, or the next day, or the next week. Months went by, a year went by, and still the little fiddle hadn't been taken out of its case. Vincent had stopped playing.

The little fiddle began to lose hope of ever being played again. Its strings broke, first one, then two, and then all the four strings hung loose. Vincent's mother once picked up the case, but only to put it still further away in a cupboard. The family moved house and the little fiddle moved with them, so it had not been completely forgotten, but it did get so badly knocked about that it was broken again.

Time had gone by, and many things had changed in the world since the little fiddle was made. There were now many cars, buses, and heavy lorries on the roads. People had radios and televisions and computers. Some of the music that people listened to had changed as well, but there were still a lot of people who enjoyed playing the same music, and they liked playing it on the instruments that people had used a hundred years ago.

The little fiddle lived in its box, high on a shelf, forlorn and forgotten. Vincent was now grown-up, with a family of his own. One day, a friend came to stay and told him about her little boy called Jacob, who had just started to play the violin. Suddenly, Vincent remembered his own little fiddle.

Immediately he started looking for it all over the house. He found the box, took out the little fiddle and showed it to his friend. The little fiddle looked very pitiful without any strings, and with a break down the side. But, even so, the visitor asked whether she could borrow the little fiddle and take it to a violin maker so that it could be repaired.

The little fiddle was made whole again. The

violin maker also gave it a fresh coat of varnish and put on new strings. There it was, all new and ready.

The little fiddle was so happy that it could be played once more. It took a bit of time to get used to having strings again and to feeling the bow on its strings. But soon it remembered how to let its body vibrate and how to make beautiful sounds.

The little fiddle now belonged to Jacob. Jacob played his violin at home and at school. The little fiddle was very excited the first time he was taken to school. As soon as it arrived, the little fiddle could hear the sounds of many other violins. Jacob took the little fiddle out of its case, put it under his chin, and joined the other players. It was then that the little fiddle looked round and saw lots of children

who were all playing on small violins – some of them even smaller than the little fiddle itself! The little fiddle knew that it would never feel lonely again.

Elena's Story

Siân Lewis
Illustrated by Penny Bell

'You know my new friend Elena?' Jane asked Miss Jones one March afternoon.

'Yes,' smiled Miss Jones.

'She won't talk to me,' said Jane. 'She's been staying at our house for two whole days now and she's still too shy to say hello. What can I do?'

'Why don't you try reading Elena a story?' Miss Jones asked. 'She might like that.'

'What a good idea!' said Jane

She knew just the right story for Elena. Miss Jones did too. She fetched the book from the back of the classroom.

'There you are,' she said with a smile. 'A story specially for Elena. Perhaps when she hears it, she'll talk to you.'

Jane rushed off home with the book in her bag. Outside the back door she could hear Elena jumping around in the kitchen. But when she tiptoed to the window and peeped in, Elena stopped.

'Hello!' called Jane with an especially friendly smile on her face.

Elena said nothing.

Jane slipped in through the door.

'Hello,' she whispered. 'Hello, Elena. Say hello to me.'

But Elena ran away. She squeezed herself into the corner between the cupboard and the kitchen wall and crouched there, quiet as a mouse, until Jane's big face came and found her.

'Hello,' Jane said, right at her.

Elena closed her eyes tight.

'Come on. Talk to me,' whispered Jane. 'Don't be shy. Look what I've got. A book! I'm going to read you a story.'

Elena heard the jingle of a satchel and peeped out very carefully. What she saw was the sun spinning in through the kitchen window and skipping on the book in Jane's hand. The pictures on the book danced like new leaves on the trees. Elena opened her eyes wide.

'Hello,' said Jane at once. 'Hello, Elena. Hell-o-o!'

At the third hello Elena shuffled her feet.

'Hello,' said Jane for the fourth time.

'Yuk!' said Elena loudly.

'You're talking!' Jane cheered. 'Good old Elena!' Her face came right into the gap between the cupboard and the wall. 'Come on,' she said excitedly. 'Say hello to me. Hell-o.'

'Yuk!' spat Elena.

And that's all she would say, no matter how much Jane coaxed her.

'All right, then,' sighed Jane. 'I'll read you a story, but you've got to promise to talk to me afterwards.'

Jane slid down into the pool of sun on the kitchen floor. She bent her head over the book so that the light shimmered on her hair. Elena watched with her sharp little eyes.

'Ready!' said Jane. 'This is for you, remember. It's an old, old story about a little starling who helped a princess.'

Elena blinked in surprise, for she was a little starling too. She tipped her head to one side, ruffled her feathers and listened.

'Once upon a time,' read Jane, 'a beautiful princess called Branwen was kept prisoner in a castle across the sea.

'Every day she had to work in the kitchen. The cook used to beat her. The servants made fun of her. Everyone in the castle was cruel to Branwen, everyone . . . except a little starling who came to her window.

'"You're the only friend I have, little bird," Branwen would sigh. "If only you could talk. Then you could take a message to the giant, my brother."

'The starling felt sorry for Branwen. He wanted to help her, so he listened and listened till at last he could speak. Then he flew across the sea to a giant as tall as a mountain.

'"Come quickly!" he cried to the giant. "Your sister is in trouble!"

'The giant jumped into the waves and walked through the sea to save Branwen. Soon she was sailing safely home, all because of her friend, the starling who had learnt to talk.'

Jane put down her book and looked straight at her friend, Elena. Elena's eyes were shining. Suddenly she stepped forward, opened her beak and whistled at the top of her voice.

'Good girl, Elena!' whispered Jane. 'You want to learn to talk, don't you, like the starling in the story. Say hello. Hel . . .'

Elena puffed out her chest and whistled her shrill happy whistle.

'No!' said Jane. 'Don't whistle. Say hell-o. Listen.'

But Elena wasn't listening. She wanted to fly to the warm sun that came dancing in through the kitchen window. She stretched out her stiff wings and jumped.

Jane whistled in surprise as the starling swooped over her head with a flutter of wings.

'DAD!' she shrieked. 'Daddy!'

Dad came running across the yard. He flung

open the door and his great dark shadow filled the kitchen.

'It's Elena!' yelled Jane. 'She's better. She's flying.'

Elena took one look at Dad and flew up towards him.

'Elena's better!' cried Jane. 'Her wing's not all floppy and awkward like it was yesterday and the day before.'

Dad reached out his hands, but Elena dodged away and perched on top of the kitchen cupboard.

'She wants to go,' he smiled.

'Oh!' Jane stopped in dismay.

Dad pulled a funny face. 'We've got to let her go now she's better,' he said. 'It's cruel to keep her locked up in the kitchen.'

'But I don't want her to go!' cried Jane. 'I

want to teach her to talk. Starlings are clever, like parrots. Miss Jones said so.'

Dad said nothing. He just slid his arm round Jane. They looked up at Elena who was watching the sun ripple through the sprouting branches of the tree outside their window. She whistled with happiness.

Jane whistled back. Elena stared down with her bright beady eyes. She hopped and fluttered and whistled again.

'I think she's saying thank you,' Dad whispered. 'Thank you, Jane, for looking after my injured wing for the past two days.'

Jane rubbed her head against Dad's shoulder.

'No,' she said in a small voice.

'No?' said Dad.

'I know what Elena's saying,' sighed Jane. 'She's saying she wants to go.'

She slipped her hand into Dad's and pulled him away from the door. As his shadow disappeared, the sun came streaming into the kitchen.

Elena shivered with joy. She let the sun swoop down her purple feathers. Then, with one goodbye whistle, she flew straight out of the kitchen door. Over the garden wall she surged, on and on until she was just a black speck in the sky.

'Maybe Elena was an overseas starling,' said Dad as the tiny black speck disappeared. 'The sort that come from colder countries to spend the winter over here. Now that spring has come, she wants to go home.' He gave Jane a squeeze. 'What do you think?'

'I don't know,' said Jane gruffly. 'Elena never said a word to me about it.'

Dad laughed. And even Jane smiled as she picked up the book from the floor.

'Read this to me,' she said, snuggling up to Dad. 'It's all about a starling who learnt to talk. It's Elena's story.'

But that night, as she winged her way across the sea to her home in Poland, Elena Starling dreamt of a different tale – the tale of a starling princess kept prisoner in a kitchen, a starling princess who'd taught a kind girl to whistle till a great giant Dad came to set her free.

That was Elena's story.

Suspicion Spreads

Folktale
Retold by Charles Vyas
Illustrated by Yabaewah Scott

When there were only animals upon this earth, the elephant was the king of all, and the hare was his adviser. The hare was very fat; the elephant was very thin.

Once the adviser was asked a question,

'Why is our king so thin?' Though the question had arisen in private, the elephant heard it. The adviser himself answered the question, 'Maybe because he is a king.'

This was also said in private, but was heard by the elephant. He thought and thought for days. Then told the hare, 'I am thin, perhaps, because I eat leaves and grass.'

'You may be right, my king,' said the hare with sympathy, and added, 'In that case, there's a way out of it.'

'How, my adviser? Tell me, how may I grow fat?' asked the elephant anxiously.

'I don't know myself, but we can seek advice from your subjects.'

'Yes, yes. Let it be so. Do not delay. Call the animals to a meeting and try to discover the cause as well as the cure.'

'That will be done, my king,' said the hare, and hurried away.

He sent a message to all the animals. The messenger announced to each of the animals he met, 'There is going to be a general meeting tomorrow morning at the king's palace. Each of you must carry with you the kind of food you eat. This will help the king to decide the answer to his problem.'

This was heard by all, including a lizard, who decided to pass on the message in his own way. He went off secretly to do this.

On the way, the lizard saw a lion to whom he said, 'Oh, Mighty Animal, the king has asked me to tell you that it is not necessary for you to attend the meeting. Instead you should guard the kingdom. What he wants from you is a piece of your skin for some magic performance, and that's why I am before you.'

The lion obeyed. He scratched off some of his skin and gave it to the lizard to take to the king.

Next, the lizard met a leopard to whom he said, 'You, humble servant of the king, you need not attend the meeting, but guard the gate. What the king wants from you is some of your spots for a special use, and that's why I am here before you.'

The leopard obeyed. He took off some of his spots, gave them to the lizard to take to the king, and lay bleeding for some time.

Then the lizard stopped an eagle flying and gave an order, 'You, the highest flier in the sky, need not attend the meeting. Simply keep a lookout for enemies and go on flying. What the king wants is one of your feathers to use in witchcraft, and that's why I am before you.'

The eagle also obeyed. He pulled out a feather and gave it to the lizard to take to the king.

After this, he approached a cat. To this animal he said, 'You, the messenger of the king, you need not attend the meeting. You are free to go anywhere you like in the kingdom. What the king wants is some of your whiskers to protect himself from the evil effects of other creatures, and that's why I am before you.'

The cat also obeyed.

When the cat disappeared, the lizard shouted at an elephant, 'You, kinsman of the king, you need not attend the meeting. After all, you are one of his family. What the king wants from you is your tusk, to give it to a two-legged being to keep him from attacking your people for ever after, and that's why I am before you.'

The elephant broke off his tusk and gave it to the lizard to take to the king.

Loading himself up with these articles, the lizard then came to the meeting and sat behind all the other animals present.

The king asked the hare to examine the food the animals were accustomed to eating and to find the type that could make him fat. The hare stood up to carry out the order. While examining the food, he came across the lizard. He asked him to show his food. The lizard showed what he had brought.

'Do you eat these things?' asked the adviser. 'If so, it's strange! Very strange! If not, you have insulted the king and you will be dealt with severely for your misconduct.'

The lizard requested the hare to hear him patiently. Then loudly he said, 'I bow to all of you who have gathered here. You have brought the food you eat. I also had my food with me, but on the way some creatures asked me to carry their food to the meeting, explaining that they were unable to attend the meeting in person. The load was so heavy that I had to drop my food in order to help them in this way.'

Saying this, the lizard began to show the articles one by one. First, he showed the lion's skin, holding it up high. Seeing this, the eland got frightened and fled. When he showed the leopard's spots, the monkeys and the antelopes shot off. Seeing the eagle's

feather, all the birds disappeared. When he held up the cat's whiskers, the doves and mice made off quickly. Lastly, he showed the tusks to the remaining audience and the king himself left the palace. As he went, the first animal he saw was the lion. To him he said, 'I appoint you king of the forest from today, to take over my duties.'

Thus the meeting broke up, but fear gripped the animals. Since then they have remained on their guard against their suspected enemies. The eland tries to keep away from the lion, the antelopes and the monkeys from the leopard, the birds from the eagle, the doves and the mice from the cat, and so on.

As for the elephant, because he gave up the worrying responsibility of kingship, he grew fat. However, he has been trying ever since to keep away from the hunters who make their living by killing his species to get money for the tusks.

Football Revenge

Julia Eccleshare
Illustrated by Yabaewah Scott

Henry hated football. He always had, and he reckoned that he always would. Luckily, no one at home expected him to like it or be good at it or even to play it. But at school all his friends seemed to think it was the best, the greatest, the most important thing in the world.

All playtime long a game of football, or even two or three, would rage up and down the playground. Anyone who didn't want to play got trampled, squashed, pushed or squeezed out of the way. The football tide flowed right up to the benches at one end of the playground and the wire fence at the other end. Even feet got trampled if you left them dangling down from the bench.

Henry was fed up. He had been trying to play transformers with Thomas and Amit and Chia when the football wave crashed over them and scattered everything.

'It's not fair,' he told Mum when he got home. 'We don't interfere with their football, but they never leave us in peace. And no one ever stops them, because football looks like a proper game.'

Mum made lots of suggestions. First she suggested that Henry try playing football. Henry groaned. 'I have tried, but I'm no good. No one wants me on their team.'

Then Mum suggested playing somewhere else. 'We're not allowed anywhere else,' said Henry. So she suggested asking the teacher.

'That's no good,' said Henry. 'Mr Taylor likes football too. He'd never stop it.'

Mum finally got tired of making suggestions. 'Well,' she said. 'You'll just have to think up something of your own.'

* * *

That night, when Henry was in bed, he did some thinking.

His younger brother Edward did some thinking, too.

'You could fight them, bash them all and tie them up in knots,' he said, and jumped up and down on the bed to demonstrate the fight, the bash and the knots.

'You could biff all the footballs into outer space.' He biffed some odd socks lying on the floor. One landed on top of the cupboard and dangled down just out of reach. The other never even made it into orbit, but dropped on to a Lego model.

'You could cover the playground with Superglue so that they all stick down and can't kick any more.' He picked his feet up slowly, showing just how difficult it is to walk or kick in Superglue.

Henry said nothing. He was thinking.

That night, he dreamed of his football revenge.

Instead of a bedside light, Henry had a globe with a light inside. All night long the little globe shone and turned slowly round and round. In Henry's dream, the globe became a football. Not a dirty white plastic football that rolled about and was kicked by anyone who felt like it, but a multi-coloured ball that looked rather like a giant gobstopper. This ball wasn't for anyone to kick. This ball was Henry's, and he alone could control it.

Henry took his multi-coloured football into the playground. He spun it in his hands and then let it stop so that everyone could see that the colours on it came from the different coloured countries on the globe. What nobody except Henry knew was that each colour produced a special effect. Touch red and a red-hot spark shot right through your body. Touch blue and it was like feeling ice – and blue was the most likely colour you could touch, as so much of the world is made up of sea. Yellow gave a jelly-like sensation. First toes, then legs, arms and finally your whole body began to feel soft, wobbly and so helpless that you would collapse in a heap. Green had the opposite effect. Anyone who touched green became still all over and creaky like a rusty robot.

Everyone gathered round Henry.

'Give us a turn.'

'Put it down. Put it down. Let *us* have a kick.'

211

'Spoilsport! It's no use to you. You can't even play.'

Hands reached out to knock the ball to the ground, but Henry fended them off. He wanted to make quite sure that his revenge would work. He did want everyone to have a kick, but only when he was quite ready.

'Teams,' he said quietly. 'Make two teams.'

There was some shouting and shuffling, and then two teams were grouped together.

'You can be ref,' they said.

Henry smiled. He threw the ball high into the air.

'Game begins,' he shouted.

Everyone rushed for the ball. Elvin's toe was the first to connect.

'Ow, ow, ow!' he shrieked. 'The ball's burning hot!' He retired to the bench.

James had fallen into a heap in the middle of the playground.

'I can't stand,' he wailed. He had touched the yellow.

Sean was wobbling in a ridiculous position. One leg was stuck out as it had been when he had first kicked. He was trying hard to get it back to its proper place on the ground, but before he managed it the other players flowed over him and he was knocked over.

Soon there were no footballers left. They had all retired from the game in a huff. Some were rubbing toes or heads which felt as if they had been stung by a wasp or pricked by a pin. Some were trying to get some feeling back into frozen fingers and toes by wriggling them and rubbing them. Some felt stiff and some felt floppy. All of them were cross and confused.

Henry trotted out and collected the ball.

'Dud ball!' Tim shouted at him. 'There's something wrong with it.'

'No one wants to play football with a rotten ball like that. It bites!' said Alex.

'How come you can hold it OK?' Darren asked.

Henry said nothing. He took the ball and put it in his locker.

The middle of the playground was empty. There was no more football. Henry, Amit, Chia and Thomas played transformers. They could go wherever they liked. Lots of games which hadn't been played for ages started up in the big space in the middle of the playground.

*   *   *

Henry slept well. He slept so well that he overslept in the morning. Mum came in to wake him up.

'Come on,' she said. 'You can't hide there all day just because of the football.'

'I don't mind about football any more. Not at night, anyway,' Henry said.

And somehow, from that day on, Henry found that he didn't mind about football in the day so much either, because however bad it was he could always take his revenge at night.

Acknowledgements

Michael Morpurgo for *It's a Dog's Life* copyright © Michael Morpurgo 2001, first published in 2001 by Egmont UK limited; the Estate of Jill Barklem for *The High Hills* copyright © Jill Barklem, first published by HarperCollins *Children's Books* in 1989; the Estate of P. L. Travers for 'Chapter 1: East Wind' from *Mary Poppins* copyright © P. L. Travers, first published in 1934; the Estate of Michael Bond for 'Paddington's Good Turn' from *Paddington Here and Now* copyright © Michael Bond 2008, first published by HarperCollins *Children's Books* in 2008; *The Wishing Fish Clock* copyright © Joyce Dunbar 1991, first published in 1991 by HarperCollins Young Lions; *Tea at Mrs Manderby's* copyright © Adèle Geras 1991, first published in 1991 by HarperCollins Young Lions; *Macaw and the Blackberry Fishcakes* copyright © John Escott 1991, first published in 1991 by HarperCollins Young Lions; *The Stonecutter* copyright © Elizabeth Laird 1991, first published in 1991 by HarperCollins Young Lions; *The Little Fiddle* copyright © Eveline de Jong 1991, first published in 1991 by HarperCollins Young Lions; *Elena's Story* copyright © Siân Lewis 1991, first published in 1991 by HarperCollins Young Lions; the Kenneth Kaunda

Foundation for *Suspicion Spreads* retold by Charles Vyas; *Football Revenge* copyright © Julia Eccleshare 1991, first published in 1991 byHarperCollins Young Lions.

The publishers gratefully acknowledge the above for permission to reproduce copyright material. While every effort has been made to trace the appropriate sources for the stories in this collection, in the event of an erroneous credit the publishers will be more than happy to make corrections in any reprint editions.

A classic collection of tales to tell children of
about four, featuring beloved characters and
lively stories, by Michael Bond, Jill Barklem
and Anne Fine amongst others, chosen by
children's book expert Julia Eccleshare.

Paddington Bear has a magical moment,
the animals of Brambly Hedge are struggling
at Dusty's mill, Lara's godmother sorts
out a noisy lion and Rapunzel is
rescued from the tower . . .

A classic collection of tales for young readers of about five, featuring beloved characters and lively stories by Michael Bond, Jill Barklem, Elizabeth Laird and others, chosen by children's book expert Julia Eccleshare.

Paddington Bear tries to buy a birthday present, the animals of Brambly Hedge set off to the seaside, a greedy queen insists on having the biggest tree in the world and will Cinderella get to go to the ball?

A classic collection of stories by P. L. Travers, Penelope Lively, Michael Morpurgo, Michael Rosen, Alexander McCall Smith and others, specially chosen for young readers of around seven by children's book expert Julia Eccleshare.

Mary Poppins takes Jane and Michael on a gravity-defying tea party on the ceiling, meet the boy who rescues a beached dolphin and can the barber keep the secret of the rajah's big ears?

A classic collection of stories by Michael
Rosen, Alexander McCall Smith, Ted
Hughes, Michael Morpurgo and others,
specially chosen for young readers of
around eight by children's book
expert Julia Eccleshare.

Mary Poppins takes Jane and Michael on a
topsy-turvy day, a boy watches over a
beautiful swan and more. . .